BLOODLIGHT

THE APOCALYPSE OF ROBERT GOLDNER

HARAMBEE K. GREY-SUN

HYPERVERSE BOOKS, LLC

ALSO BY HARAMBEE K. GREY-SUN

Standalone Stories

Beholder

Love Among the Ultramoderns

The *EVE OF LIGHT* Series

<u>The Novels</u>

BloodLight: The Apocalypse of Robert Goldner (*Prequel*)

Broken Angels (*Book I*)

Divinities, Entangled (*Book II*)

<u>The Short Stories</u>

FoolKillers

The Lark

Heaven's Gun

Knotty & Ice

Rogue Beauty

Deviant-Hunter's Sabbath

BY HARAMBEE GREY-SUN

Poetry

Spring's Fall (Autumn Numbers * Book I)

Wine Songs, Vinegar Verses

Print ISBN-13: 978-1-64044-907-7

Ebook ISBN-13: 978-1-64044-908-4

Third Edition: February 2018

Cover design by Phillip Gessert

Published by HyperVerse Books, LLC

www.hyperversebooks.com

Crossing genres without apologies.

PART I

———

ENTANGLED

1

One false move and the snow warriors would kill him. Robert couldn't escape this feeling. He couldn't escape *them*.

He'd broken free from the cheerleader tug-of-war between Suzi and Debbie, and fled from the entire teenaged party crowd at Brian's house, clomping fifty feet or more through the snow, heading—he thought—to his Mustang. But space and time in his mind blinked, and he somehow ended up in the middle of a maze of seemingly undead snow creatures.

The revelry in the house behind him rattled windows almost to the point of shattering them, and all the noise fed his vision of a frozen-over personal hell: him lost amid dozens of swaying snowmen and snowwomen, the latter outnumbering the former. Most of them were a few inches taller than his six feet, but all of them were armed.

Part of him knew these were simply snow-and-wood sculptures, not alive at all. Their stick arms rubber-banded with other sticks so each seemed to hold a wooden sword, or a spear, or a gun. He really had nothing to fear. And yet, as he maneuvered between them, another part of him swore these things could do him serious harm if he wasn't careful. The broken beer-bottle fragments acting as nipples on the snowwomen nurtured this belief.

He couldn't reason with them, nor could he wrestle them down. The only useful skill left was his skill with geometry, but he couldn't think straight for more than a minute at a time. He tried to keep an arm's length distance from each one; half-arm's length was the best he could do. Try as he might to watch their trembling tree-limb arms, he couldn't help but gaze into the cat's-eye marbles acting as their eyes as he passed each one. Nor could he help but consider the absurdity of their form: their robust snow bodies, white like bone, and their skeletal wood arms, brown like his skin. Half alive, half dead.

Through sheer dumb luck, Robert emerged from the thicket of snow warriors after what seemed like an hour. But he was still unsure of his sanity. On the white and uneven ground in front of him, he saw the snow warriors' elongated shadows shifting in rhythmic movements to the pulsing music coming from the house behind him. *An orgy*, he thought as he watched the shadows, his among theirs. *A violent one.* Not so long ago, it wasn't just shadows on the ground.

He shook his head and turned around. That fucking party. The riotous noise shook not just the house's windows, but its entire structure, including the back porch lights, accounting for the shadows that really moved and the snowfolk that just seemed to. That was rational. He needed a good dose of rationality to chase away his more fantastical ideas. But just how the hell had he ended up among the snowfolk in the first place? Had he stepped into a wormhole? Or had he been so lost in his own thoughts that he'd wandered around blindly?

He chuckled. Thank fortune no one on the wrestling team saw him wandering around like an idiot. They might figure he wasn't fit to represent them at the tournament next week. The team knew he didn't drink or do drugs, so they'd no doubt take his behavior as a sign of him going nuts. It was fine to go crazy on the mat, within the rules, but off of it, the wrestlers had another reputation to uphold.

Robert chuckled again at his temporary bout of goofiness, and then he saw it: PARADISE LUST. Partially obscured by the shadows of low-hanging, snow-stressed branches, the sign gave a title to the art exhibit from which he'd just escaped. It looked like someone else was upholding their reputation.

In all the years he lived in Wallace, Virginia, Robert had never experienced the record snowfall as seen during the last week of January. He figured the moment it was safe to come outside, Brian's prurient little brothers had taken advantage and constructed the latest in their unending series of disturbing masterpieces. Graffiti artists, garbage sculptors, and overpass banner hangers—those two thirteen-year-old snarks had talents and visions well beyond their years. Presently, Robert just had a headache. The evening had started out fun, but as it progressed and more and more girls had come up to him—whispering in his ear, grabbing his biceps and other muscles, promising favors he definitely didn't need or want—it had devolved into confusion.

Brian always threw the best house parties. And the worst. He and Robert went all the way back to third grade. It was an extremely rare feat to keep such a friend through the purgatory of middle school and into the junior year of high school, especially when they went to different schools, so Robert had felt obligated to attend the Valentine's Eve party. But he wasn't obligated to accept everything that fell into his lap, blew on his neck, or tugged at his wrist; he was never doing that again. He'd tried to bail, but somewhere between the house and the car, he was plucked and placed in the exhibit. Now free, he tried again, trying to reorient himself in Brian's unreasonably large backyard. Having upper-middle-class friends could be such a pain in the ass.

He plodded through the snow like a man playing human

checkers against himself. They must've been smoking some serious weed back in the house, and he was undoubtedly experiencing a considerable contact high. That was another probable reason for him ending up in the middle of the exhibit, and a very good reason to leave the party early—if after midnight could be considered early.

While stumbling, Robert looked up at the full moon, bright and slightly blemished. He saw something phenomenal encircling it, something at first glance so unbelievable yet so beautiful and amazing it made his eyes glaze over. The spell broke, though, when he heard something moaning behind him.

He stopped walking, shocked that something else alive was out in this weather and a little afraid of what it might be. He turned around slowly. After a little more moaning, he located its source. Just beyond the reach of the house's lights and hidden from moonlight by branches, a figure lay curled up in the snow.

Certainly not a victim of the mock battle of snow warriors, the person may've been wounded in some other fight, possibly a victim of a beating who'd tried to make it to safety but failed. Or maybe it was a drunk who'd ambled aimlessly through the woods and collapsed when entering the clearing. As he neared, Robert concluded it was most likely a con man, waiting to perpetrate a sick trick—robbery, violence, rape—upon any passerby naive enough to approach too closely and give the Samaritan passkey: *Are you okay?* If that was the case, he was ready to handle himself.

As he came within a few paces, however, he sighed and unclenched his fists. He wasn't the only brown-skinned wrestler who'd lost his way in the snow. Robert snickered before speaking.

"Uh, Davin, my man…that isn't how you make a snow angel."

It was, however, a sure way for the sixteen-year-old to get sick. Davin tipped the scales at just over one hundred pounds when wet, and here he was in only his boxer shorts, socks, and a ripped T-shirt, lying on his side with his knees almost touching his forehead, his arms crossed and pressed close to his body, both hands clutching his chest. He wasn't shivering. He wasn't even moving. But he was conscious. Robert's joke drew a groan in response.

He stared at the clenched eyes and the grimace on his friend's face, his relief and good humor plunging into concern. He then looked around for missing clothes and saw a sweater, stretched all out of shape and hanging from a tree branch several feet away. The dress shirt Davin had been wearing under it had been ripped off and was lying on the ground near something that glinted—a belt buckle—which had somehow become separated from the belt. He saw no sign of Davin's belt, pants, or shoes.

He knelt down to put his hand on Davin's shoulder. "What happened, man?"

Davin moaned.

"Can you speak?"

A grunt this time.

Robert didn't smell any trace of alcohol, so he ruled out the possibility Davin had gotten drunk and engaged in some kind of party-animal dare. He noticed scratch marks on his arms and legs, and someone had obviously tried to rip his T-shirt off. But if this was the result of a fight, it had been a strange one. Excluding his own, the only other relatively fresh footprints nearby indicated one person who'd come from the direction of the house and stumbled near the edge of the woods before collapsing and rolling into the heap that was Davin.

A breeze nipped at Robert's face. *Act now and ask questions later.*

Robert picked him up and carried him around the side of the pulsing house toward his car; he couldn't help but notice that his friend felt lighter than he should have. Robert weighed 159 pounds and benched 260. Still, Davin should've felt closer to a sack of sand than a sack of Styrofoam in his arms. Yet another question for the list. He considered a hospital, but Davin's home was closer. Hell, it might not be that serious anyway.

After carefully laying him in the backseat of his Mustang and spreading a blanket over him, Robert paused to look up at the sky before getting into the driver's seat. It was still there. A set of seven concentric circles, each a unique color, encircling the full moon. Was he the only one who saw them? Were others outside, looking up on this early Valentine's morn, taking it as some kind of portent? *Fuck it.* Right now he had to see to the safety of his friend.

Robert sped off toward Davin's house, praying his parents wouldn't assault him with questions for which he had no answers.

EVEN THOUGH ROBERT didn't drink at the party, lack of sleep after the stress of dealing with Davin's mom did no favors for his head. After just three hours of rest, he woke up with a very faint but distinct buzzing sound lodged somewhere in his cranium, initiated by his alarm clock but not silenced even after he unplugged and tossed the damn thing. Now pushing through one of his school's side entrances, the morning buzzing bloomed into a pounding headache. Out of bed and into bedlam.

Howard Phillips High School's social landscape wasn't much different from central Virginia's other public high schools. There were jocks and mean girls, preppies and rednecks, geeks and motorheads. All run-of-the-mill for a twenty-first-century American public school with a student population just over one thousand.

But there were also the eccentrics, those who may've been unique to schools in the mid-Atlantic region, or maybe even just unique to Howard Phillips. Like the five brawny Jewish guys who could've dominated the football team if they'd had any interest in sports. They shaved their heads bald every morning and covered their pates with red, white, and black yarmulkes. The skullcaps' designs resembled targets, and they were nothing less than dares to the sneering rednecks and the feverish evangelicals who couldn't resist doing a double take every time they passed. Robert was friendly with a couple of them and was pretty sure none of them were particularly religious, but the five felt they were in enemy territory and refused to bow or keep to the corners. He admired the hell out of them for that.

Jewish skinheads aside, there were other kinds of skins: those guys and gals who wore as little clothing as they could get away with. Autumn, winter, spring—it didn't matter. The stripteasers weren't shy, but neither were the teasing onlookers who thought each of them should spend at least one day a week in the gym.

And then there was the slumber party: those kids (mostly stoners) who came to school dressed in whatever they'd fallen asleep in, usually either sweat suits or flannel pajamas. Robert was waiting for one of them to show up in nothing but boxer shorts and a robe; he'd once made a bet with Davin on whether they'd get away with it.

When the United States Heartland Security Agency was created a few years ago, in that chaotic period following the President's murder, odd effects rippled through all levels of society. At the lowest levels, some public schools saw some of the nuttiest results. Robert guessed the confused adults running the government wanted to keep the wheel spinnin' by instilling the same confusion about rights and wrongs, dos and don'ts, in those who were on the cusp of adulthood. Guns had been outlawed for the general populace, but it was still mandatory for public schools to have metal detectors. Cigarettes and marijuana were legal (the hard age limit being eighteen, while the shake-the-head-but-look-the-other-way limit was sixteen), but possession on school grounds meant an immediate five-day suspension. Students were generally allowed a little more freedom of expression when it came to fashion, but there was still a dress code. Shoes, boots, or sandals were mandatory. Hats and nonreligious head coverings were banned. No individual could show off more than two tattoos at a time. And a display of racist language on one's skin or clothes was a definite no-no—though Robert had noticed no one ever seemed to get in trouble for homophobic slurs.

He'd dressed in his usual way this Monday: sweatshirt, sans names or logos, and blue jeans, sans holes, patches, rips, or decorative chains. Unusual when compared to the fifty other African-American students' styles. Just a few days away from seventeen, he was long past the age where he gave a damn about fitting in.

He weaved through the in-crowds and out-crowds, neglecting eye contact with them all. Not a one of them intimidated him in the least, but his jack-hammering headache kept his thoughts out of focus, his body a little off balance. It was only when he was a few steps away from his locker that he realized he was being followed by that unique clique of one: Leigh, the only girl in school who wore a striped or polka-dotted bow in her hair every single day. She'd apparently been yipping at his heels as he walked—for how long, who knew. She and her words only came into focus when he stopped in front of his locker and faced her standing in front of hers, two doors down.

"How in the *hell* could you go to a party without me?" she said, shaking her finger in his face. "Without even *asking* me?" Her fingernails were painted black, with a cherry-red dot in the middle. A black bow with dark red polka dots tied up her hair on the left side.

In personality, Leigh had come a long way from the freckled and four-eyed dishwater blonde who'd caught his eye during a junior high field trip to the zoo; tall for her age, and appropriately clumsy, she'd almost fallen into the wild dogs' pit while the rest of the class was several feet away, listening to a lecture about zoo safety. He didn't flinch to rescue her. He just saw and laughed, never speaking to her until their freshman year when she confronted him about the incident, her bluish-gray eyes staring deep into his brown ones. *Why did you just laugh and not try to help?* The confrontation coming a year after the fact was a shock, as was the confession of her long-held secret crush. At the time, he was hurting from a personal tragedy, and her attention—her affection—was like a potent medicine: effective, but dangerous. The danger was in him being black, her being white, and them living so near the capital of the undead Confederacy. Virginia was changing, but racist ghosts still roamed.

Now the glasses were gone, the freckles were less prominent, and, at six feet, the girl had mastered her body's movements. But this was still Wallace, Virginia. And the girl still owned her share of goofiness. She insisted on going to the extreme in color-coordinating her outfits, and taking it further on special occasions. Like today. Neither her voice nor her black-and-cherry Valentine's Day getup was doing any favors for Robert's head.

"We're supposed to be girlfriend and boy—"

"Shhh!" Robert raised his hands, as if his shushing alone would be ineffective.

"We are *supposed* to be dating," Leigh said even louder, as Robert winced, "but no gift, no surprises—except the fact that you can't even take me to a Valentine's Eve party!"

It took a moment for him to digest just what she was going on about. Then he fell into guilt-defense mode. After a few stuttering attempts, he managed to spit out: "What Valentine's Eve party?" He then grimaced as something jabbed, sharply, from inside his skull at his right temple.

"Don't lie. Don't even *start*. Florence said she saw you there."

Robert snorted. "Florence seeing things...as usual. Everything but the glowing, growing nose on her makeup-caked face." Even as he was saying it, he noticed but couldn't prevent the weird poetic phrasing.

"Shut up and answer me," Leigh said. "Why didn't you tell me you were going?"

"I *wasn't* going...I mean, I didn't mean to go. And I didn't stay. I was only there briefly. Davin's sick. I spent much of the night with him and his parents." Now he rambled, involuntarily, but at least closer to his usual manner of speaking.

"Bull! Florence said—"

"Screw Florence! That girl is seventeen years old and still doesn't even know the entire alphabet! You can't trust her to construct a complete proper sentence, let alone trust her to say anything close to the truth." From incoherent fragments to an unfiltered rant—he wondered if that was progress.

For a moment, Leigh seemed ready to defend her friend, but the shifting expression on her face showed she thought better of it.

"If you don't believe me," Robert said, "ask Davin's parents."

"No."

Robert smirked. "Because you know I'm telling the truth."

"No," Leigh said. "Because I'd look like an idiot calling two adults I don't even know to ask about you."

"Well, then, you just have to trust me."

"I'd definitely be an idiot if I did that."

Robert rolled his eyes then frowned as the hall began to empty at the first-period warning bell. "We're going to be late for class. We'll get in trouble."

"Be late. You go anywhere before we're finished and you'll be in trouble with me."

At the beginning of the school year, Robert thought it fortunate their lockers were so close in proximity. He thought much differently now.

"Tell me straight," Leigh said. "Honestly and clearly. Why didn't you take me, of all people, to the party? What, was your dad there?" While they both intended to attend law school after finishing college, only Leigh already acted like a prosecuting attorney, cross-examining without mercy some hapless witness for the defense. "What can *possibly* be a good excuse for not taking your girlfriend to a Valentine's party?"

"'Cause that ain't the point of Valentine's Eve parties, cooch!"

Robert turned at the sound of the voice, though he really didn't want to. It was an irresistible urge, like looking at a car wreck. Herman was a one-man wreck. A do-rag wearing, grinning, six-foot-three example of everything a young black kid shouldn't be. The obnoxious fool was wearing the even more obnoxious jacket that had the phrase "Gutta Step" prominently displayed on the back. He'd apparently been watching Robert and Leigh spat from nearby and decided to get closer to the action, undoubtedly to make things worse. At least he was alone, for once; his fellow Gutta-Step boys were nowhere in sight.

"Valentine's Eve parties aren't for couples," Herman said. "They're like bachelor parties set in a whorehouse. You go to get away from your hitch, and hook up with a bunch of hos. Once it's over, you come out, repledge your heart to your ball-n-chain, and pretend it never happened. That's the *real*, shorty!"

Leigh looked at Robert with eyes that wanted to shoot bullets. "So that's how it was!"

He wasn't sure why she was directing all her anger at him rather than the guy who'd used at least four sexist terms in less than two minutes.

"That's how it *wasn't*," he said. "Brian's party was nothing like that...while I was there."

"That's not what I heard," Herman muttered.

"Shut up, germ," Robert said. "You weren't even there."

"But you were!" A stamp of her foot further punctuated Leigh's words.

"But I—" The first-period final bell interrupted Robert's words and exacerbated his headache. He covered his ears with his hands.

"Fine," Leigh said. "Shut me out now, but we're not finished." She grabbed his locker's door and slammed it. He hadn't even had a chance to get his books out.

Leigh hurried away toward class as Robert fumbled with the combination lock. His first period was health, which, fortunately, the head wrestling coach taught. The coach wouldn't give one of his star wrestlers extra work or even a hard time for showing up late—at least, not during school hours. Robert knew he'd probably have to run a few extra laps around the gym after practice that evening, but he never minded extra exercise.

Herman leaned against Leigh's locker, smirking as Robert tried his best to ignore him. He opened his locker to grab his book and folder, glancing down the hall in time to see Leigh turning a corner and disappearing from sight—most of her anyway.

At the corner where she'd turned, the colors of her ebony-and-red outfit hovered in space, forming a vague outline of her body. The edges of the image blurred into the background scenery of steel lockers and painted bricks; still, Robert could clearly make out the shoes, the pants, the belt, the top, and even the buttons on the top, not to mention that stupid polka-dotted bow. Without an actual body to fill out the image, it appeared two-dimensional and, for a moment, the image simply shimmered, like glitter covering the surface of a wall of water, flowing but going nowhere. In a blink, however, the image developed another dimension, appearing as if it truly did have a body. Its "legs" and "arms" swung as the image "walked" toward the intersection of the two halls and moved a few paces toward Robert before stopping.

He refused to blink as the "clothes" peeled off, dropping into a heap at the "feet" of what remained standing: a skeleton, comprised of "bones" that were shafts of pulsating orange and indigo lights. The thing stood rooted as its left "arm"—pulsating faster than the other shafts—rose into a gesture that looked as if it were offering something to him.

His eyes dried as he stared at this bright appendage. He considered whether he should blink or, lest he miss something, keep holding off for just a few seconds more.

"I see you're still listening to that gay shit."

The words jerked his attention to Herman, who was focused on the picture taped to the inside of Robert's locker door: cover art for an old Psi-Kyll Soul CD. He sneered at Herman and looked down the hall again. There was no trace of the image.

"Homo. No wonder you can't get anything better than that pale scarecrow."

"Go suck yourself, you—" Robert stopped himself. He didn't have time to engage in a verbal battle with someone as witless as Herman. He grabbed the books and folders for his second- and third-period classes and, not caring for his headache, slammed the door, holding a faint hope Herman would stick out his hand and get his fingers caught. No such luck.

Robert turned to jog to class, but a green light flashed in his eyes. He stumbled, dropping a book as Herman chuckled.

"Valentine's Day is a real bitch for you, isn't it?" he said. "Just like your girlfriend."

Robert grabbed his book and hurried away, wondering when would be a convenient time to stop by the nurse's office for some aspirin—not that she was legally permitted to dispense anything, even over-the-counter stuff, but she sometimes hooked certain students up, those who knew how to ask nicely. He did his best to ignore Herman trotting behind him and making goofy sounds, but when he opened the classroom's door and Herman ducked out of sight, shouting, "Happy V.D.! Ho ho ho!" Robert wished he'd just decked the guy back by his locker.

Mr. Myers stopped midlecture as everyone turned to see Robert standing in the doorway, his face contorted with embarrassment and rage. Herman was now halfway down the hall, laughing behind Robert's back while most of the class laughed in front of him. Myers looked pissed.

Robert closed the door and trudged to his seat, calculating the number of times he'd be forced to circle the gym.

2

Robert wondered why he'd even bothered to come to school today. At the very least, he should've skipped advanced biology. His temples hammered, breaking his clear thoughts into shards. And Mr. Sailers did what he could to stain those shards with his usual environmentalist theology.

"It should be obvious by now," Mr. Sailers lectured, "to anyone with eyes to see, and a mind to comprehend, that we humans are a suicidal species. Homicidal and suicidal. We give more abuse and visit more horrors upon our environment—our generous nurturer—than we heap upon ourselves. We seem to be *sick*. It is no wonder some philosophers have equated human beings with a disease spreading, crawling on and under the skin of the planet Earth, living off of the planet to its detriment."

There was no way this was appropriate for a public school setting, but Robert would be the last to protest. Outside of calculus and physics, he got his highest marks in biology. But today, did he have to suffer abuse from without as well as from within?

"The discovery and perfection of our ability to make fire was the beginning and end of modern human civilization," Mr. Sailers said. "We're inconsiderate, careless creatures who don't think or plan much beyond dusk. Seeking only to acquire what it takes to engage in carnal pleasures in the dark, we forget the Earth turns, new light comes, and with the return of new light, we see, dimly, that our nighttime actions have destructive consequences for the near future."

Enough.

He wasn't sure of his headache's source, but the pinch in his rear, prompting him to stand and head for the door, was conscience. And shame.

The hallways during third period featured only a handful of sleepwalkers—those who were cutting class but unsure of where to go or what to do. Their numbers usually increased after the lunch periods. Robert was rarely among them. He couldn't go home, and he didn't want to go anywhere else. He'd a brief thought of hopping in his 'Stang and going to the nearest pharmacy for something stronger than aspirin, but anything stronger could interfere with his acne medication. Rather than head for the exit, he climbed the stairs and headed for the second-floor window overlooking the parking lot.

Leigh had parked next to him. Or had he parked next to her? If the latter, it was a mistake. He was in such a damned fog today, but one thing was clear: that dent on his passenger's side door wasn't there yesterday. Even from this distance, he saw the red paint in the dent's groove. Red in black. Leigh's Volkswagen Beetle was fire-brick red. Her outfit today was ebony and red. "Black and cherry," she'd said at some point this morning when he was hearing but not listening. She'd been hinting.

Davin had once hinted. During that one crazy, *stupid* time last year he'd talked Robert into going to a "party" hosted by some girls he knew in the city. Davin knew from the outset "party" was a euphemism for "orgy." Neither participated at first; they just watched, pointed, and commented. But Davin took a few tokes of something and was soon getting into it. Robert had wanted to leave, but he got caught up in the mood, in the haze; it wasn't too long before he got caught up in a tangle of arms and legs. After some time into it, when his and Davin's shoulders happened to brush, Davin leaned over and whispered. He had an idea...and it turned into a mistake, one never spoken of or hinted at again. But Robert saw it in the cracks of anything incongruous, read it between the lines of anything poetic, heard it in the breaths that were the pauses between misspoken words. The mistake wouldn't escape him.

It struck him again last night when Davin's mom—the only parent home at the time—looked as if she wanted to strike Robert. She stayed her hand, but not her mouth, chewing Robert out left and right as she worried over Davin's unconscious body. *What'd you do to him? Why didn't you take him to the hospital? What's wrong with you?* The last thing she said after placing Davin in the minivan was, "It was a mistake for you two to ever be together." She then slammed the driver's door and sped off for the ER.

In the parking lot below, a few cars down from his, two girls were leaning against a Camaro making out. Robert sighed. They were asking for it. But maybe they couldn't help it. Maybe one of the girls was like him. Every other step he took was a mistake. How could it be otherwise? *He* was a mistake.

He'd known it for years, ever since his five-year-old self had wandered from his bedroom to the living room where his parents were hosting one of their wine-night get-togethers. He innocently asked his parents to keep it down. In return, his mother blurted out her guilt while spilling red drops on the cream-colored carpet. She'd never wanted a damned kid. She'd never wanted to be a damned school nurse. She'd wanted to be a jazz singer. Unwanted and unplanned, Robert had ruined her life. And Robert's dad, a "towering bully" in her words, had ruined her life.

And both of them were ruining her life at that moment, trying to stop her from speaking her mind, trying to stop her from telling her wine-party audience what she really thought about herself and about them. The damned men in her life were trying to stop her from saying all the things she could never take back.

Even at that age, Robert understood mistakes; he made them all the time. It seemed he couldn't get out of bed without doing so. What he didn't understand was the anger behind his mother's words, the rage behind her eyes when she looked dead into his. Maybe he wasn't meant to understand. He sure as hell never saw that look again, nor did he ever hear her use that tone of voice. After that night, his mom and dad never drank again, not even a sip of bubbly on New Year's. His mother never got angry at either of them again. She spoiled them both, often unreasonably, until she was gone.

Robert wasn't about to go back to class. He wasn't in the mood to take another minute of Mr. Sailers's crazy rants. He stayed at the window, letting his gaze drift from the parking lot to the football and soccer practice field, coated now with at least two inches of hardened snow. His mind followed the lead of his eyes, drifting this way and that, as they regarded the sun rays filtering through the gray above to dance with the snow's diamondlike crystals. He saw shimmering apparitions here and there; the thoughts nearest and dearest in his mind shaped them into vague outlines of human figures. It was a party, with two figures standing out among the others. His mom and his dad, dancing...fighting...plotting...whatever. A murder of crows descended on the field and shattered the entire reverie.

Damn, those are big birds. Big black birds on a sea of white. Had someone scattered crumbs out there? Had the birds seen something else appetizing that Robert couldn't? A half-buried rat's carcass? They didn't seem to be pecking for food. They weren't even walking or hopping around. Their beaks and their eyes were all oriented in one direction—Robert's.

Shit.

He turned away and shook his head. From last night's snow-warrior incident to this morning's light skeleton to *this*. It all had to be a side effect of his new acne medication; that was the latest and most plausible theory. At least the pounding in his head had finally gone away. He'd take hallucinations over headaches any day. Still, he could do with a splash of water in the face. He walked to the nearest restroom.

Shit, again. Wrong room.

Howard Phillips was a relatively peaceful high school. It was nothing like the war zones in the city. Still, it was a public high school. Each hall corner, each section of the parking lot, each lunchroom table, and each bathroom belonged to some clique. Robert was cool with many and didn't give a shit about most; he generally went wherever he pleased. But there were some groups that didn't give a shit about him either. There were even some in those groups who would've loved to kick it out of him, given the opportunity. Wandering into cutter territory alone, Robert had just given them one.

Mostly white, with two or three light-skinned Hispanics, the cutters were body-art enthusiasts. Tattoos, piercings, what have you. They were also total assholes. In class, they often wrote obscenities and slurs on their palms, flashed them to friends or foes, then licked off the evidence with a studded tongue. Their main reputation, however, rested on knives and razors, the blades everyone knew they carried but that no teacher or security guard could ever find. They passed through the metal detectors each morning without so much as a blip. And they always passed the pat-down test. And yet, whenever they needed it, they always seemed to be able to slip a razor blade from under their tongue or pull a knife out of their ass.

Of the seven boys in front of Robert, the five youngest tossed their cigs into the urinals and flicked switchblades at him. The two who were Robert's age gave him the stink-eye but kept right on puffing.

Robert gave the stink-eye right back to all of them, not even flinching at the switchblades. His flight response was rabbit-punching his gut, and his fight response was crouching somewhere in his backside, but his head fought both instincts. He'd do what he came to do then leave. He turned an indifferent shoulder to the menaces as he walked toward the middle sink.

"You lost?" Nate asked before taking another puff of his cancer stick.

"No." Robert turned the cold water knob. "But I think you are." Nate was actually an honors student. Both he and Hank, the other boy who kept on smoking, were in two of Robert's classes. Hell, Hank was the vice president of the French Honor Society. The two were smart, and "cut-ups" in more ways than one.

"Oh yeah?" Hank said. "We're in the men's room. This ain't the place to powder your nose."

"Maybe not." Robert splashed a second handful of water into his face and turned around. "But it might be a good place to paint yours red."

Two of the knife-wielders stepped closer, both of them fresh-men, one of them muttering. "Jig..."

Robert looked him in his eyes. "I'll be happy to dance. On your broken neck." He didn't want to fight—his *head* didn't—but he stepped closer to the boy, his instinct kicking him in the ass.

"Hey...*hey*..." Nate, the nicotined voice of reason, held up his hands and took a step closer to the boys, ready to save them from themselves. "Not today. Not this day." A sentimentalist, not wanting to see his buddy get his nose split on Valentine's Day.

But it appeared the freshmen didn't want to go out like punks. Not around these older boys. Not when most of them—they hoped—had their backs. They stopped advancing but continued to brandish their knives. Robert could see it in their eyes. Tough fronts, but they really didn't want to take it further.

Robert glared for a moment then turned to spit in the sink before walking out. He wasn't sure why he'd done it, but the gesture had felt right. He was sure they'd gotten the message. And they'd gotten his blood hot. He'd be clenching his fists, trying not to pound his desk for the rest of the day, just waiting until wrestling practice. He hoped stress wouldn't make him explode before then.

3

———

In spite of the freshman wrestlers' mop-up-and-wipe-down session over the weekend, the practice room still reeked of odors other than sweat and cheap cologne. It was a wonder that practicing three hours a day, six days a week, for almost every week since mid-October in the dim and humid padded box hadn't made any of them permanently ill.

Nearing the end of Monday practice's first hour, the wrestlers worked on routine setups, takedowns, and throws as Robert wondered whom he could trust to take notes for him in physics on Thursday and Friday. He'd be out both days, attending the regional wrestling tournament, and normally he'd count on the one and only object of his trust in the class: Leigh. But after their earlier confrontation, he'd experienced a gnawing sense of worry. Most of Robert's physics classmates were diligent note-takers, but reluctant when it came to sharing. And even though the teacher was fond of Robert as a student, he was also hostile toward anyone who would prioritize athletics over academics. It was unlikely he'd pull Robert aside and tell him what he was going to miss in class while he was seventy miles away, "fooling around in some other school's gymnasium."

As he executed a single-leg takedown on his partner, Robert had both a good idea and instant regret: Take Leigh out on a surprise date this week. A belated Valentine's Day gift and an apology. *Romantic and brilliant*, he thought, *but equally impossible.* Between practice and homework, there was just no time. And how exactly would he surprise her anyway? In a way that didn't blow up in his face?

He'd skipped lunch to go buy a ten-dollar Valentine's Day card, slipping it into her locker before the period was over. She was probably surprised to discover it, but not pleasantly. After seventh period, Robert found its shreds at the bottom of his locker.

"All right, now counters!" Coach Myers made an extra effort to be heard over the heavy metal music blaring out of the nearby CD player. "Work on your counters to takedowns now…Let's go!"

Robert shot in for a double-leg takedown on his partner, Rusty, who sprawled, deliberately falling forward while kicking his legs back, almost collapsing on Robert's neck while applying pressure on the back of Robert's head and shoulders with his hands and hips.

Robert grunted, "Shit! What're you doing?" as Rusty spun around and got behind him.

"*Counters* now, Rob," Rusty said. "Pay some attention and stop doggin' it."

Those thinking Rusty's red hair was his most prominent trait quickly changed their minds when hearing him speak. He sounded like someone with permanent laryngitis who was always shouting to make up for it.

Robert shook his head and grumbled as he got up and positioned himself in his standard wrestling stance. Rusty quickly shot in for a double-leg takedown. Robert forgot to counter and forgot to move until the force of Rusty's shoulders caused him to stumble backward while falling forward. Rusty didn't wait for

Robert to remember his role, but simply dumped him on the mat—hard.

"Damn, man!" Rusty said, springing back up to his feet. "What's the matter with you? Get into this!"

"You two stop *screwin'* around and do some *goddamn* work!" Coach Myers screamed at them from the far corner of the room.

"C'mon," Rusty said as they got back into position. "You haven't even worked up enough of a sweat to wash that ash off'a your legs. Hell, you're rustier'n I am!"

"Then let's forget the rust and see how much *red* I can beat out of you." Robert grabbed Rusty's right arm and shot in quickly for what was to be a fireman's carry takedown, but—as Rusty prepared to counter—it transitioned into a duck under, with Robert ending up behind him, keeping a firm grip on Rusty's left wrist and elbow.

Robert used the element of surprise to obtain momentary control; he planned to pick Rusty up and throw him down to the mat. But he hesitated. This gave Rusty plenty of time to break free of Robert's grip and go in for a low single-leg takedown on him.

"Nice try, Robbie," Rusty said as Robert fell to the mat, "but no dude's ever goin' to get *me* from behind."

Rusty scrambled to his feet. Robert tried to spring up just as quickly, but a sharp, fleeting pain in his groin stopped him. Rusty offered his hand in half-mocking, half-sincere aid. Robert took it without thinking, and without thanks.

Rusty snorted as they got into their stances. *Here we go*, Robert thought. A snort from Rusty was always a prelude to some comment intended to provoke a bullish reaction from someone.

"Y'know what I never got about black people?" he said as they circled each other.

"Everything?" Robert snatched at and caught hold of one of Rusty's wrists.

"No, their hands." Rusty twisted his wrist loose from Robert's grip. "How it's all like white people on the palm side and all dark on the other side." He grabbed Robert's left wrist. "What in hell's that all about, huh?"

"It's to confuse and confound idiotic shits like you." Robert freed his wrist and circled quickly to the right then the left, trying to get a side view of Rusty for a good attack.

"Yeah, y'know, it's really like what they say." Rusty kicked his leg back and kept it free as Robert attempted an ankle pick. "You're just tryin' to make yourselves white, secretly, a spot at a time, rubbin' your hands and feet together."

Robert knew this ploy. Rusty would always begin and charge on with racial taunts when he felt Robert wasn't working hard enough. It was only intended to fire him up—nothing more, he was sure. The two of them had known each other since fourth grade, back when Rusty still went by his birth name, Russell. And even though, like many of their teammates, Rusty openly and proudly referred to himself as a "redneck," Robert had always judged him as being absent of any real racist feelings, noting that one of Rusty's personal deities was Jimi Hendrix. But Robert was also no stranger to naiveté.

He'd no problem keeping up with Rusty's trash talk. He was skilled enough to give better than he got. When it came to skills on the mat, though, he and Rusty were much more evenly matched—except when Robert was distracted.

"You're right." Robert snatched hold of Rusty's left wrist. "It's all part of our grand plan to go undercover, and seduce your women under the bedcovers with us."

"Our sisters and daughters, huh?" Rusty twisted free and grabbed Robert's right wrist.

"Yeah, well, not *your* skanky sister," Robert said. "But your slutty mother on the other hand..."

Rusty swung his free hand—curled partway into a fist—at Robert's head, to either punch him in the jaw or set up a head-lock throw. Not taking any chances, Robert ducked under Rusty's arm while getting his own wrist free in order to reclasp Rusty's, getting him into a body lock. Not pausing for a breath this time, Robert lifted him up and threw him down to the mat in one flowing motion. With Rusty lying on his stomach and Robert lying on his back, he let go of Rusty's wrist as he applied more and more pressure. He wanted to pin Rusty to his back.

But as Robert hesitated, deciding on which pinning combination to use, Rusty shifted his leg and brought his knee closer to his chest. Within seconds, he'd gotten his body into a prostrating, base position. Applying the full weight of his body to Rusty's back, Robert frantically tried to regain wrist control, now realizing he never should've relinquished it—a freshman's mistake.

"Take your laps!" Coach Myers shouted as the two assistant coaches at the opposite ends of the room blew their whistles.

Most wrestlers scrambled to their feet, ripping off their headgear and flinging it into the nearest corners as they dashed for the door, heading for the school's main gymnasium to take three laps around the perimeter. Robert wasn't among them. He was usually among the first five in the sprinting pack, but having been thrown off Rusty's back and nearly onto his own at the first word of Coach Myers's command, he was one of the last out of the door.

He began among the heavyweight-class stragglers comprising the back part of the group, which stretched into two then three separate groups as the faster and fastest runners hit their stride. He barely managed to catch up with the middle group, making himself the object of Coach Myers's jeers each time he passed him standing on one of the lower bleachers.

"Goddamnit, Goldner! Stop being a pussy and get your ass up there where you belong!"

He tried, but just as it seemed as if he might actually make it into the first group, Robert saw everyone in front of him walking toward the exit. He'd already completed all three laps. He slowed to a stop as Coach Myers shouted.

"Make it quick! Get your damn drinks and get back in the damn room, ready to wrestle!"

Winded—though not enough to stifle chatter and grumbling—the wrestlers ambled down the hallway and into the auxiliary gymnasium for a few quick sips at the water fountains and a short bathroom break, one of two they were allowed during practice.

On the gym's floor, the girls' basketball team sat in a semi-circle around their coach, who was calmly lecturing them on what they needed to do to continue their winning streak to the state championships. While waiting his turn in line at one of the fountains, Robert wondered why the girls weren't practicing in the empty main gymnasium. The boys' basketball team had it unofficially reserved for after-school practices during the entire winter sports season but the boys were nowhere to be seen. Why not take advantage of their absence? Had the girls just been trained too well to know their "place"?

At least they're allowed to practice out in the open, Robert thought, *even if it's off to the side.*

The cramped, stuffy wrestling room was in an area of the building students jokingly referred to as "the basement." Even though the area was actually on the school's main floor, it just happened to be in the same area as the special ed and shop classes.

He looked at the girls in the semicircle. It was about an equal mix of blacks and whites. He tried to imagine himself among them, wondering how different his path would've been if he—the mistake—had been born a girl. Would he have bothered with a sport at all? And would he have chosen basketball, or would the stereotype—that orange watermelon—have scared him off?

As he was, nothing had scared him off from the expectation of wrestlers to submit themselves totally to the great cult of wrestling, forging trinities of mind-body-spirit. They were expected to become visibly bruised during every practice, make their opponents weep in pain or humiliation after every match, and rouse the audience to scream at the top of their lungs at every meet. All the while, they were to say nothing, just wear a stolid mask as the coaches urged them on to a sweaty and grimy —if not bloody—victory on the mat. Afterward, they were to condition and think about nothing but the next match, even if it was half a year away. *"Never go to your back,"* Coach Myers often screamed. *"Learn to sleep on your stomach!"*

The head coach of the girls' basketball team encouraged his players to focus their minds on life's greater pleasures during the off-season: art, music, literature, nature's unified beauty. Contrary to making them soft, this method probably strengthened the mind and spirit far better than any gym could. During the season, the team's main objective was to *be* artful and beautiful, to work like nature's clock, always succeeding. And they did so in an almost supernatural fashion. But like nature and great art in modern society, they were ignored by the masses. Robert knew they were truly a rare crew. At rival schools, average-looking girls with top-level athletic skills comprised the girls' basketball teams. At Robert's school, the girls looked more suited for the cheerleading squad, yet they were impelled by who-knows-what to perfect their initially average playing skills. It wasn't long before the young women regularly displayed supernal skills on the court, looking wonderful to most observers while doing it, and winning game after game—far more than expected or, some whispered, fair.

If Robert had been born a girl, he was sure he'd be fundamentally the same. Even if lucky enough to land on the girls' basketball team, despite the different surroundings and conditioning, it wouldn't be enough to fix him.

He reentered the wrestling room. As always, he had to blink several times while his eyes adjusted to the poor lighting. Still blinking, he retrieved his headgear and spotted Colin. Davin hated the guy and made no secret about it, but Robert always argued with him that blacks on the wrestling team had to stick together, look out for one another. For what purpose he wasn't exactly sure, but it just felt like the right thing to do in this environment.

He sat next to Colin to stretch.

"Hey," Colin said, as he lay back in slight arching position, stretching his stomach muscles, "you wanna go with me first?" Colin's eyes gazed toward the ceiling, but Robert knew he was speaking to him.

"Go where?" he mumbled as he stretched his groin.

"No 'where,' dumb-ass." Colin turned to face him. "We're doing matches next. Those of us wrestling this weekend. I heard coach talking earlier."

"You know he's going to be the one to pair us up, you shit." Robert refocused his stretch to his shoulder blades. "Why're you even asking me? You know how it goes: lowest weight class on up. And we'll have to wrestle the scrubs before facing each other."

"Not this time," Colin said. "Coach is pissed Davin's not here today. So he's going to take it out on those of us who *are* here. The guys who're wrestling this weekend are all wrestling each other. Full matches, our choice of partners. Then we wrestle the scrubs on J.V. And *then* we wrestle each other again, coach's choice. Then full-court gym-sprints, I think. No slow-go. It's all nonstop for us, win or lose."

"Bullshit." Robert stood to stretch his calves. "Nobody can wrestle straight for that long, with that many different partners."

"Oh yeah?" Colin said. "You make it sound like an orgy."

"All right!" Coach Myers entered the room. "Everyone wrestlin' this weekend, pair up and choose a circle. *Now*, damn it! Get your asses up and *move*! We're going full matches, and *none* of you better let yourselves get put on your back! Everyone else, stand up at the walls."

Coach Myers blew his whistle. The freshmen, junior varsity wrestlers, and varsity-level losers of last Saturday's district tournament cleared off of the mats and took their positions at the mat-padded walls. Colin ran to the center of one of the circles painted on the floor mats near the room's center. Robert walked to the same circle, studying Colin's face, wondering what he knew. Had Davin said something?

Coach Myers turned off the CD player by smacking it on its side as he passed by, walking toward Colin and Robert. The assistant coaches stepped into position to referee the other two pairings.

"Ready?" Coach Myers grunted with the whistle between his lips. Colin and Robert hurriedly shook hands and resumed their wrestling stances. *"Wrestle!"* All three coaches blew their whistles.

Colin immediately shot in for a double-leg takedown. Alert and ready, Robert sprawled, putting his hands on Colin's head and shoulder. Without taking a breath, he spun around to get behind while grabbing Colin's left wrist, pulling it toward his waist, and applying pressure on Colin from behind with his hips. Colin tried to stand up and reverse, but Robert, holding his left wrist firmly, grabbed Colin's right elbow with his free hand and exerted one quick burst of pressure forward, forcing Colin to lie flat on his stomach.

That was the easy part. Robert then tried a variety of pinning combinations, but Colin countered each one, eventually getting back on his feet.

"Escape, that's one," Coach Myers grunted. "Points're even now, you two."

Colin fussed with Robert's head, planting his hand on the top and trying to push or pull it, shove or drag it to one side in order to get Robert to look away for just one second, just enough time for Colin to take another shot. Robert used his forearms to fend off Colin's intrusions long enough for him to play the same type of head games. All the while, the two circled each other, attempting or faking setups, locking up briefly head to head, only to wrench free again while staying tunnel-focused on each other, sense of sound tuned to nothing but their own coach-referee's whistle and comments.

"Goddamnit, quit stalling!" Coach Myers barked at them. "Somebody better take a goddamned shot, *quick!*"

Robert did and managed to take Colin down again, right before Coach Myers blew his whistle.

"That's time for the first period," he said.

Robert let go of Colin and they both stood up, quickly returning to the center of the circle. During the entire two minutes of the second period, both seemed possessed by the spirits of Olympian deities as they tussled. Robert was still ahead by two points when the period was over, but the score had increased from 4–2 to 10–8. It wasn't until Coach Myers blew the whistle and they disengaged that Robert realized his sweat-soaked T-shirt was spotted with what appeared to be blood. He quickly checked himself for cuts. At an official wrestling meet, the match would have been paused on account of bleeding. In practice, one had to wrestle until the match was over.

In the thirty seconds he had before the start of the third period, Robert didn't find any broken skin, but he did notice glittering red specks on the back of his hand—these in addition to the usual red welts on his biceps and forearms that always resulted from grappling on the mat. Colin had to be the source. Robert hadn't noticed anything on him while walking to the water fountains earlier, so Rusty wasn't suspect. In his cursory examination of Colin's T-shirt and exposed skin, however, Robert couldn't see any evidence of cuts or rubbed-off scabs. Colin's sweat-drenched shirt was a uniform beige color from front to back, no red dots or blotches, and his arms and legs showed only old scars.

On his hands and knees, the standard base position for the losing wrestler, Colin waited for Robert to kneel and assume his position behind him. Robert stepped closer and slowly began to kneel, but he stopped and made a diamond-shaped hand signal to Coach Myers indicating he intended to let Colin go free to neutral standing position. The coach nodded at Robert and gruffly said, "He's letting you go, Jenkins." Colin maintained his position as Robert leaned over and, still making the diamond signal, placed his hands on the area between Colin's shoulder blades. "Ready?" Coach Myers asked. Robert glanced at the specks on his hands before looking back at Colin's legs and feet. The whistle blew.

Colin punched high and stepped out, attempting to stand, turn, and face Robert in one smooth motion. Robert attempted to stop him by reaching his left arm around Colin's waist while his right arm reached for Colin's right ankle, but the exertion triggered a yellow flash in Robert's eyes, stunning him, stopping him before he could get a firm grasp on the ankle. The effect lingered, forcing Robert to blindly grope for his intended targets. His right hand hit the mat twice, quickly in succession. His left hand, hovering near Colin's navel, made one wide reach for the right side of Colin's ribs; instead, it found the lump of flesh between his legs.

"Damn!" Colin shouted as Coach Myers blew his whistle. "You fuckin' cocksocket! Get *off* me!" Using little wrestling skill or technique, he did what he could to get away from Robert as he stood up.

No longer seeing a depthless mass of yellow—just black with random yellow splotches—Robert let himself be fended off as he released all holds, held his hands up near his head, and fell back on his rear.

"Goldner, what the hell are you doing?" Coach Myers shouted as the whistle fell from his mouth to dangle by its string.

"Shit, man..." Colin had moved way away from him. Robert could tell by the sound of his voice that he was probably pacing just outside the circle.

"Shut up, Jenkins!" Coach Myers said. "Walk it off! What the hell are you doing, Goldner? Grabbing nuts will cost you a match!"

A few of the reservists lining the walls laughed. Shawn, the biggest and most vocal of the freshman wrestlers, even whipped off a few antigay quips.

"You four think it's a joke?" Coach Myers bellowed. "It's funny? Go take five laps...*Now!* And you better be back here in five minutes, ready to wrestle. *Go!*"

Robert heard several footsteps move quickly toward the door as he stood up. By the time the door slammed shut behind the runners, he'd regained most of his vision.

"Sorry." He hung his head and blinked at the few twinkling, swirling yellow dots that remained. "Sorry, man," he said as he reentered the circle.

Colin mumbled to himself.

"My...I..." Robert stammered for an excuse to give before remembering the wrestling team's uncompromising motto: no excuses. It was a convenient remembrance. He wasn't able to produce anything acceptable anyway, motto or no motto. *I went temporarily blind. I went temporarily insane. I went gay, temporarily.* Any of those statements might as well be another.

"You're giving up a point, Goldner," Coach Myers grunted as he put the whistle between his lips. "It's ten–nine. Get into position, you two."

Colin reluctantly got back into the standard base position. Robert stared at his back, not sure he wanted to touch him, not sure he could trust his eyes or hands.

"Get into damn position, Goldner!" Coach yelled.

Blanking out all objections, Robert again made the diamond shape with his hands and placed them on Colin's back. The whistle blew. Colin exploded up as before. Robert let him stand.

"Escape! That's a point," Coach Myers said. "You're even."

The two circled and physically taunted each other as they had during the first two periods. They made setups. They attempted and faked shots. They tied up briefly, headgear to headgear, before releasing. Neither one was able to gain any momentary opening.

Finally, Robert snatched both of Colin's wrists. Before flinging them aside to shoot in for a takedown, he glanced at his hands. They were tingling. His glance became a stare as his fingers unclasped their grip, straightened, and wriggled in all directions. Robert felt nothing. His hands had gone numb. But he saw the fingers—long, thick, brown, sweaty, *slimy*—blindly twisting this way and that. Worms, testing out the environment into which they'd just emerged.

He gazed at the writhing digits until the index finger-worm on one hand and the middle finger-worm on the other straightened out, stretched their respective lengths by an inch, and suddenly recoiled, *bent* back so that the tips of their blind heads touched the back of his hands. Robert gasped and pulled his arms away as Colin took advantage, shot in for a takedown, and brought Robert down to the mat.

Colin began positioning himself to execute a pin when Coach Myers blew his whistle. "That's time!"

Colin sprang up to his feet, hustling to get to the center of the circle. Robert remained dazed, flat on his stomach, staring at his hands, now balled into fists. He uncurled his fingers slowly. Nothing appeared strange now. The ten digits had bones and were jointed. Even the glittering red specks from earlier were gone, presumably wiped away during subsequent tussling with Colin. Nothing was there but sweat, skin, hair, and nails. Everything seemed normal.

He returned to the center of the circle and shook Colin's hand firmly while looking him in his eyes.

"Good match," Colin said. "Just watch your hands next time."

Robert said nothing as they released and headed toward the door for a lap around the gym.

"Hurry it up!" Coach Myers yelled after them. "Come back ready to go again! New opponents!"

Robert wasn't sure he'd be ready to go again so soon, new opponent or not. Seeing stars after getting thrown to the mat or coming up too fast was enough to deal with during a fast-paced match. How would he handle it if, during this weekend's tournament, he suddenly saw a new universe and his hands again became subject to its strange laws of physics?

4

R obert pushed the peas and mashed potatoes around his plate, just like he was five years old again. He sure felt like a child, unable to fully understand all that had been happening to him over the past twenty-four hours.

His father stared across the dinner table at him. Neither had said a word since grace. Only the soft notes of a saxophone and a chant about the supremacy of a certain kind of love wafted from the kitchen, underlining the silence, until his father finally spoke.

"Janice called."

Robert looked up from his plate. His tongue, seemingly numb from nonuse, had trouble with his response. "Ja—? Davin's—? Wh-what'd she say?"

His father took his time chewing his meatloaf, looking straight at Robert the entire time. Not a good sign. Swallowing, he laid down his silverware, wiped the corners of his mouth, and cleared his throat. "Davin's in the hospital. One run by the HSA." A terrible sign.

In the chaotic wake of the First Lady murdering the President all those years ago, there was only one thing everyone could agree on: the world was in a dangerous state of instability. The

Heartland Security Agency was founded to help prevent American society's collapse, and the first thing they did was to establish their own health care facilities. The HSA's nearest hospitals were in Richmond and just outside of D.C. There were at least five or six regular hospitals closer to Wallace, Virginia, but the highly secure facilities were for special patients only, those vaguely considered an unspecified risk to others. Patients weren't released unless they were either dead or the government deemed them good and ready to reenter society.

Robert swallowed and asked, "For how long?"

"I couldn't get much from Janice. I'm not sure she has any information to give."

"Damn," he muttered.

"*Not* at my table, Robert."

Hell, what other reaction should he have? A mere "darn it" would've mocked the situation. His closest friend may as well have been in a penitentiary. And, of course, Janice wasn't going to give his father any useful information. She was a light-skinned woman; in America's darker days, not too long ago, she would've been labeled a "quadroon." She didn't care much for dark-skinned blacks and, as a result, Robert's father didn't care much for her. The two were cordial with one another, but certainly not friends.

"What exactly happened last night?" his father asked. "Just what were you boys doing?"

"I wasn't doing anything except trying to avoid the degenerates. I hate those...stupid parties." Robert shoved the spoonful of mashed potatoes into his mouth. "I'm about through with all of them."

"Was Davin drinking too much?"

"I don't know. I don't think so. He didn't smell like it."

"You didn't drink anything, did you?"

Robert put his spoon down and looked his father in the eyes. "Dad, come on. My medication..."

"I know all about your medications. I also know the dermatologist told you to do several other things that you don't seem to be doing."

"No need." Robert resumed with his potatoes. "The new pills made the pimples go away. There are still some blemishes but—"

"See?"

"*But*, they don't burn. They don't irritate me."

"Well, they irritate me. Free health care, free prescriptions, free advice—it seems the least you could do is follow it. Now—"

"Nothing's free," Robert said. "I hope you're not teaching your students anything different. Kids come out of elementary school messed up enough as it is."

His father grunted.

"And I'm *not* wearing that body cream stuff. The one time I did, all my partners at practice complained. And coach screamed at me. More than usual. It makes my skin sticky, and I can't have sticky skin. It's against the rules and I could cost us a match."

"You don't have a match every day."

"You wrestle in practice like you would in a real match. No slow-go, as coach says. It was bad enough when I started taking those stupid acne pills and they gave me gas. The wrestling room smelled even worse than usual, and everyone knew it was me."

His father sighed and shook his head. Robert looked back at his plate to get another spoonful of potatoes, but hesitated. Against the lumpy, off-white background, he saw several black specks hovering over his food. He gazed for a moment, half-expecting them to zigzag in the fashion of flying insects and half-expecting them to land on his food to begin their meal. They only hovered. Robert waved his free hand over his plate. They darted away, then came back to hover. He waved again. The specks fled then flew back. His father stared at him for a minute before asking, "What are you doing?"

"These gnats won't get away from my food."

"There aren't any gnats in here. This place is spotless. I make sure of that."

"But—*look!*"

"You're not changing the subject." His father wouldn't even glance at Robert's plate. And when Robert looked again, the specks had gone. "I still want to know what happened at this party. Brian's a decent boy, but those other knuckleheads he runs around with...You know, there's a reason I avoided taking a decent-paying position out in the city."

"So I could go to a school overrun by white rednecks instead of one overrun by black thugs?" Robert asked rhetorically as he sprinkled pepper on his peas. "Good move."

"Watch that mouth. Did anyone start anything last night?"

"A fight?" Robert asked. "Not while I was around."

His father snorted. It was a few seconds before Robert picked up on it.

"Not because I'm a tough guy or anything," he said, "but because I went out of my way to avoid any ruckus."

"So Davin was off to himself, never bothered?"

"When I saw him, he was talking to Trixie and laughing his butt off."

"Trixie?"

"Tracie Johnson. I...uh, the guys..." Robert cleared his throat. "She's popularly known as 'Trixie.'"

His father sighed again as he raised his glass to his lips. "And then what?" he asked after swallowing a sip of orange juice.

"Then, nothing. I saw him a few more times after I first got there, around ten o'clock. He was in good spirits. Walking around. Socializing. Then, after the balls dropped—"

"*What?*"

"When it strikes eleven at these parties, it's called the dropping of the..." He caught himself, and trailed off into a cough. "Well, everything changes. The music, the mood, the atmosphere. The idea is to 'let it all out,' express yourself to the fullest before midnight. I don't know why. I think it's supposed to lead to a greater appreciation for midnight, the changing of the date, or something."

His father shook his head and mumbled as he raised his glass again.

"The deejay at the party put on this really fast-paced Caribbean music," Robert said. "Brian turned on all these strobe lights and police-car lights he'd set up around the room, and everyone started dancing, screaming and hollering, and jumping around. I tried to get into it at first, but I just couldn't take it. So, I went upstairs and chilled in the kitchen for a while. Davin may've been caught up in all of that craziness. I didn't see him again until I found him outside."

"I don't want you to go to any more of those parties," his father said after swallowing. "Janice is extremely upset."

"What does that have to do with me? I didn't do anything— I'm the one who found him and took him home!"

"I know. And the Andersons appreciate it. So do I. You were raised properly, but some of those other fools at the party obviously weren't. Davin is hurt, maybe seriously. Thank goodness, the Andersons belong to the same health care program that we do. And whatever happened, happened at Brian's. I'm not necessarily blaming him, but his parents are a little too indulgent, a bit too trusting. Or negligent. I wouldn't be surprised if the Andersons try to sue them."

"Huh, yeah, they could use Leigh's mom. *That'd* be a good introduction." Careless. As soon as he said "introduction," Robert wished he could de-introduce what he'd said. Any mention of lawyers or their practices automatically conjured up images of either Leigh's mother, an attorney who went to law school right after Leigh was born, or Leigh herself, who intended to go right after she graduated from college. His father knew neither. And he had a funny little household rule about knowing all of Robert's friends.

"Lee?" he asked. "That someone else on your team?"

Robert blinked at him. "...Yeah...and a darn good entangler, too..."

Lee versus Leigh. A boy's name winning over a girl's. His father would probably only make that mistake once. Robert shoved another spoonful of potatoes in his mouth. If his father caught the obvious trick of him trying to avoid the subject, he didn't let on. He instead went on with his meal, giving Robert time to think, not about Leigh, but about what else his father said.

"*Damn* it!"

His father almost choked. "Robert!"

"Sorry, I was just thinking about Davin. He's supposed to wrestle this weekend, at regionals. If he's too sick to wrestle, coach is going to be pis—" Robert caught himself this time. "Extremely unhappy."

"If he's any kind of decent, caring human being, he'll put concern about someone's health and well-being far ahead of concern about some athletic competition."

"Well, he's a man. I'm not sure about that caring and decency stuff." He shook some extra pepper on his peas. "We have, or *had*, seven people qualify for the regional tournament this year. A new record. Davin, Colin, and I were the only blacks. Now it's up to Colin and me to represent properly, and Colin will probably lose. He's got some tough opponents in his weight class."

"It's always up to you represent properly anyway," his father said. "In anything and everything. Will never be any different."

Robert sneezed, three times, in rapid succession.

"Bless you," his father said.

Robert opened his eyes and began with "Thank y—" but ended with gazing at the dozens of black dots swirling, orbiting about his head at different speeds and in various directions.

He didn't know how long he stared, but when he began

swiping and swatting, he did so furiously, muttering all sorts of words.

"Robert, I told you to stop with that language," his father said. "And *stop* spreading those other germs, too. What's the matter with you tonight?"

"Look at—! These—!" The dots amassed in groups of five, seven, and ten, zigging and zagging before zipping toward his ears. In seconds, the air was clear. "I—" Robert sniffed and looked about him for any trace of the horde. "Sorry. I just keep seeing..."

His father furrowed his brow and looked Robert in his eyes.

"I don't know what's gotten into you," he said, "but when wrestling season's over, you'd better remember how to conduct yourself properly at the dinner table." He stood and carried his plate to the sink. "The dishwasher's broken again, so wash them by hand. After you wash your hands."

"Okay," Robert said with a sniffle.

"And don't forget to take out the garbage after cleaning up."

Of course he wouldn't. Not tonight. That had to be what was attracting all those damned gnats.

5

———

Lunchtime was pretty much the only time Howard Phillips could pack so many cliques into one large room without a scuffle breaking out. Pep rallies had been banned two years ago as they inevitably degenerated into mini riots; forcing all students into an enclosed area, even one as big as the main gymnasium, and asking them to scream and shout for whatever reason, was just begging for trouble. School "assemblies" were now conducted over the intercom with the students seated safely in homeroom. But the cafeteria wasn't a trouble-free zone. On average, there was one verbal or physical confrontation every seven or eight days, notwithstanding the five security guards lining the walls. Any student wanting to avoid getting caught in the crossfire had to take the room's social temperature and choose his seat wisely.

Robert had taken the temperature, but after loading up his tray, he remained almost frozen, turning only his head to survey his options. He was already in deep shit. Sitting at his usual table could sink him even deeper.

The majority of the wrestling team sat near the wall. Leigh and her...*their* friends and acquaintances sat closer to the center of the room. Student council members, honor society officers, and some of the more academically inclined athletes—that table was where he really belonged, one of the few where he could sit and feel relatively comfortable. But probably not today.

Students sorted themselves according to shared passions and ethnicities, and they sat accordingly. It was no surprise most cliques turned out to be ethnically homogenous; the school was 85 percent white after all, and hardly anyone, including Robert, gave a damn about forced integration. If even the black and white evangelicals refused to sit next to each other, what could anyone do? And yet, popularity trumped all. If one was lucky enough— through either good looks or high achievement—he or she was assumed into the heavenly mass that lorded it over all other cliques. Student council officers, cheerleaders, football and male basketball varsity players, and those too cool or beautiful to sit elsewhere populated the two longest tables at the exact center of the lunchroom, making sure all the others saw who truly ruled the student body. Accompanied by Suzi or Debbie, the school's only two black cheerleaders, Robert occasionally sat among them; that is, when he had the stomach to endure the conversations without getting nauseous. He rarely had the will. The basketball team's varsity players were also part of the "Gutta-Step Crew," the small clique of black male students who proudly repped themselves as the ultimate "playas" when dealing with women. Two members of this odious crew brushed past him now on their way to their reserved spots.

"Hey man," Martin's lips almost contorted into a sneer as he spoke. "You gonna come sit with us today?"

"Nah," Herman answered for Robert. "Goldnerd can't hang with us today. He needs to go over and patch things up with his cabbage-patch bitch. That scarecrow *thang*."

Robert sighed as the two walked on. Their table wasn't even under consideration today. And although Leigh's smaller table was also one of the few truly welcoming of both genders and all ethnicities, he was sure it wouldn't be so harmonious with his presence. Not with Leigh still pissed at him. Even though they publicly pretended they weren't an item, when Leigh got mad at anyone, she made a scene; the security guards would only laugh at this one. Robert instead went with a better bet for peace, choosing a true display of unity by sitting with the team —*his* team.

He walked swiftly and stiffly, careful not to even tease a glance in Leigh's direction. It was unlikely she'd do anything other than scowl or make an obscene gesture, but if any of his other friends at her table met his glance, they might motion for him to join them.

Robert reached his seat without his neck weakening and received nods from a few of his teammates, most of whom were listening to Darren recount the details of his previous season's matches.

"That guy was a complete puss," Darren said. "I could've rolled that sonuvabitch straight to his back in the first minute of the first period. But, nah—I *owed* him. Back in junior high, this fish, floppin' around on the mat, not knowing nothin' about wrestling, chipped my tooth. And then, all this time later, he acts like he's never seen me before, like he doesn't remember nothin'! Well, hell—I was sure gonna make sure he remembered me. I was gonna stomp a mudhole and put a hurtin' on this bastard!" Darren laughed as others at the table chuckled and grinned in empathy. Robert only forced a crooked smile as he sipped his milk.

Darren had transferred from a school in Kentucky last fall and made immediate friends with most on the team when he'd joined. Robert kept him at an arm's length when he could. Here was a kid who insisted on differentiating himself from the teams' avowed rednecks by openly referring to himself as a "hillbilly." He even wore overalls to school. Robert wasn't sure why, but he suspected it had something to do with the joke he'd once heard

Darren make about "East Coast rednecks bein' too liberal about who they're pallin' around with." Never mind that Virginia—especially Wallace, Virginia—was far more Southern than East Coast, with his affected and annoying drawl, Darren never let his teammates or anyone else forget where he was coming from.

"It's like that guy from Central I went up against," Greg said. "'Member him?"

"That dancin', jive-talkin'"—Kenny paused as he glanced at Robert—"brother?"

"Yeah, that one who ran his mouth when we saw 'im at the mall, when he had all his bros with 'im. I couldn't *wait* to face him! I made damn sure I ripped some of that pubic hair off'a his head before I was finished with that fish!" Laughs went around the table again as Robert slid a forkful of green beans into his mouth. "On our feet, this guy just kept hoppin' and slidin' around. When I got 'im down on the mat, he couldn't do shit! He just lied there! Someone shoulda told this bunny long ago that the jungle boogaloo ain't a good wrestlin' move!" More laughter. Robert had a comment, but he swallowed it with his green beans. He now remembered why he usually preferred to sit at Leigh's table rather than here, and it had little to do with her.

He wasn't offended by the fact Greg had a Confederate license plate on his jeep—hell, about half of the school's rednecks wore Confederate flag belt buckles—but he didn't take too kindly to the fact that, on the one occasion he'd offered to give Robert a ride, Greg insisted he sit in the back. Allegedly, only Greg's girl-friend was allowed to sit next to him.

"Hey Goldner," Kenny asked, "what happened to Davin? I heard he's sick."

"*Sick?*"

"What?"

"He'd better not be—"

"We *need* him—"

"—*both* you guys this weekend!"

It seemed story time focusing on "Wrestlin' Wit' Sambos" was over. Now that they were concerned about a *brother* who might be useful to them, all eyes were on Robert. He chewed his food slowly as he looked around the table, waiting for everyone to settle down enough so when he did speak, he'd be heard.

"Don't worry," he said, after swallowing. "He's sick, but he'll probably be back and ready to wrestle by Thursday." An outright lie that was meant to calm had the contrary effect.

"*Prob'ly?*" Greg said. "What the—?"

"What are you talking about?" Kenny raised his voice above all others. "What's wrong with him?"

"I don't know." Robert tried to sound nonchalant, even though he knew he was more worried for Davin than any of his teammates.

"Flu's going around."

"He better not have *that* shit," Greg said. "Not now. No *way*."

"Coach is gonna be—"

"Look!" A switch flipped; Robert wanted to toss his fork at one of them. "Coach is going to be pissed, yeah, but then he's going to say that you all should stop acting like a bunch of little runny-nosed cowards, stop acting like a bunch of fussy pussies, stop *acting* altogether, and *be* the goddamned men you think you are, knowing that—with or without Davin—we can still walk out of this tournament with six winners, a new record for the team! What do you think coach will say about that? Now c'mon—if you care about Davin, care about *Davin*, but don't start crying like we're all down and done like an evening sun. We still have something to accomplish."

Robert wasn't sure where that down-and-done-sun stuff came from, or why his attitude flipped so suddenly, but he knew passion was a hell of a feeling, conjuring up all sorts of weird wordplay.

Greg pounded his fist on the table. "That's right!" The others nodded and muttered their agreement before turning their attention back to their food.

"I sure hope you step it up this weekend," Darren said, between mouthfuls.

"I always step it up." Robert gazed at him with a glacial expression, strong enough to freeze any follow-up comments. It worked. Then someone shouted from the lunchroom's center.

A black kid was standing with one leg raised high off the ground and waving his arms over his head. He appeared to be mocking the common sounds—if not the common gestures—of a woman having an orgasm.

Robert sighed. Herman, again. Bugs Bunny in blackface. A grinning loony coon. Herman was the premium ammunition— no, the atom bomb—for any at Howard Phillips who wanted to insult or look down on blacks.

Most of those seated near the center of the room cheered Herman's performance with raucous laughter. At Robert's table, Kenny simply said, "Why doesn't that monkey sit down and shut his mouth?"

"Watch it," Colin said.

"Watch what?" Kenny said, in an almost convincing tone of innocence.

"Calling us monkeys."

"I'm calling *him* a monkey," Kenny said. "Not you."

Robert wondered why Colin didn't speak up before when Kenny and Greg were going on. He knew the reason he kept his own mouth shut. Herman *was* acting like an animal. He almost always acted that way in public. Speaking against Kenny's comment would, in this case, be the equivalent of speaking a lie against his own honest thoughts.

"Just watch it," Colin said.

Kenny dropped it, but Greg picked it up.

"I'm watchin'," he said. "I'm watchin' some asshole jive around with some rag on his head, and those teachers over there—

Johnson and Zimmer—ain't doin' a damn thing. But when we try to put our hats on after school in the halls, we get yelled at and threatened with suspension. I'm *sick* of all these bullshit double standards."

Colin debated, but he was outnumbered at this table. And with the likes of Herman being used as the majority side's Exhibit A, he couldn't possibly muster anything but a weak argument.

Robert tuned them out as he chewed his food and eyed the "Gutta Step" on Herman's jacket. *How can anybody defend that with a straight face?* he wondered. He already knew the defense for Herman's green-black headwear. When he first started wearing it in early September, Herman *was* approached by a teacher and told to remove it. He refused. In the principal's office, he cited religious reasons for the head-rag and later produced a note to prove it. Robert continued to see him in church every Sunday morning after that, just as he had for the ten or so years previous; so, other than the faint possibility of Herman moonlighting as some Eastern cult's convert, Robert couldn't fathom the religious reasons behind the rag. In fact, he'd noticed from the start how suspiciously similar the rag looked to the ones worn by members of Herman's favorite hip-hop group, Da Booty Duty Crew—and he knew there was nothing religious about those idiots.

Robert turned his attention back to his tablemates, almost immediately wishing he hadn't.

"And I bet *he* was the one the librarian caught fuckin' under that staircase by the gym!" Greg said. "And he wasn't even suspended!"

"You don't know that was him!" Colin was nearly yelling at this point. "You don't know *who* it was!"

"I know they were black!"

"That's bullshit!"

"It's *all* bullshit," Rusty cut in. "No one was havin' sex under any damn stairs. That story's just a myth. Didn't happen at all."

"How do you know?"

"How do *you* know?" Rusty said. "Did you see anything? Were you there?"

"Were *you*?"

Several needles jabbed Robert around his left eye. The rapid and precise pain began just under the outer tip of his eyebrow and ran over the eye, curving down at the bridge of the nose, and continued under his lower eyelid. The needles stabbed, then stopped, jabbed, then stopped—a steady pulsating pain forcing him to wince every few seconds. The pain was so intense he was unable to tell whether it was on or under the surface of his skin.

The pain then switched to his right eye, stabbing and jabbing with the same frequency as before. The pins attacked five or six times before switching back to the left eye, accompanied by a throb in his left temple. Suddenly switching back, a throb in his right temple matched the attack around his right eye.

"Will you all just shut up?" he said.

They all ignored him as his side-switching headache increased in intensity.

"I said shut up, goddamnit!" Robert banged his left fist on the table as he shouted. On impact, a dark green light briefly engulfed his fist. His tablemates apparently hadn't seen. They'd definitely not heard him shout as they kept on arguing.

Robert raised his fist, now unsure whether he'd just imagined the green light. It was still smarting from its collision with the table, but the backside of his hand was fine. His knuckles were fine. He uncurled his fingers. His nails were the shade of forest green.

Robert held his gaze, unblinking, until the bell rang, signaling the end of the period. Startled by the noise, he balled his hand back into a fist and, just as quickly, uncurled his fingers again. Incredulous, he blinked twice. His nails had returned to their normal hue. He took a long breath as he clutched his lunch tray and joined the others filing toward the tray racks.

Now vigorously debating with Kenny, Darren, and Greg over interracial dating, Colin grabbed his tray and jerked up from his seat; he almost dropped it when he turned and bumped into a kid passing behind him.

"Watch it, you white piece of shit!" Colin snapped.

"Oh, *excuse* me, bro!" The gangly, long-haired kid smirked as his crew laughed and continued on their way. All of them pale and sporting unkempt hair, ripped and bleach-splotched jeans, and stained denim jackets with the names of various death metal bands scrawled on the back.

"Fuckin' metalhead," Colin said before continuing with Greg, Darren, and Kenny as they headed toward the lunch tray racks. "You guys need to look at the *real* world. Stop just looking at the pictures—"

Colin's words and his debate opponents' responses mixed in with other voices and became indistinguishable in the din of the exiting crowd. Robert kept his distance from them all, wondering how soon he could set up an appointment with his eye doctor—after wrestling season was over, of course.

6

When he took the garbage out after dinner, Robert saw a corona—the seven colors of the rainbow, encircling the full moon—just as he had on Valentine's Eve. His thoughts inevitably turned to Davin.

He was still in the hospital. Robert's father had spoken to Janice just before dinner, but there was no new word on Davin's condition. He was still just "sick" and, of course, not allowed to have any visitors. At least, that was all Janice would say. Was it her or the Heartland Security Agency that was refusing to pass along more information?

One thing Robert did know was that his coaches and teammates were less than happy to have one of their best wrestlers fall sick at such a crucial point in the season. One of the best in the team's recent history. One of six blacks on the wrestling team, varsity and junior varsity combined. And one of how many gays?

He'd often wondered, ever since Davin confided in him late in their sophomore year. Robert and Leigh had been going through a rough patch at the time; so rough, Robert considered their relationship as one between a "scarecrow" and a "crow," the imagery borrowed from Herman's repeated mockery. Leigh had seemed to be pushing him away, and Davin's secret was intriguing. But Davin also had to maintain the front, had to be seen flirting with girls, even going so far as to make out with girls at an orgy, until...

Robert shook his head, dropping the bag of garbage into the bin. It was darkly amusing that many male adolescents—ranging from the brainy to the dim, from the athletic to the awkward, from the popular to the peripheral—regarded anyone who wrestled as a "queer." And yet the members of the wrestling team, almost without exception, were among the most macho, fearsome males in the entire school, regarding any other males as pussies pretending to be men, whether they played sports or not. And then there was Davin, one of the toughest and the most respected on the team. As far as Robert knew, no one suspected anything, but contemplating it all now—contemplating where he and Davin had gone together—made his head swim.

He glanced up at the cloud covering the moon as he entered the garage, thinking about the pressure Davin had to constantly endure, from without and from within. Perhaps the opposing sexual and intellectual forces had finally taken their toll on the poor guy. Or maybe it was less complex. Maybe someone found out his secret and decided to come at him in a cowardly fashion, perhaps by slipping something into his drink at the party. Attacked by one's own broken conscience or the lack of one in someone else. Whichever, the result was the same.

Robert went into his room and turned on his laptop. He only had calculus and economics to work on, so he could do his homework while listening to music—thankfully. He didn't have the presence of mind to concentrate on reading or writing tonight.

He clicked through his catalog. As usual, he'd gotten enough jazz during dinner. And he wasn't in the mood for blues—why make himself even more depressed? He decided instead on an always-welcome favorite: Psi-Kyll Soul's first album. He plugged in his earbuds and sat at his desk.

The first song, "Alone Again, Beautifully," provided the

perfect notes. Each note acted as a bright foot-track for each step his subconscious took down poorly lit tunnels, over obfuscated bridges, and through dim labyrinths constructed by the calculus problems he was examining. He never had to put too much conscious effort into a math problem, just enough to begin the deconstruction as the rest of his thoughts flew to dwell on whatever. He tried to force his thoughts off Davin, off wrestling, and off school as he concentrated on the music and lyrics.

He'd first heard one of their signature songs, "Time—Untie Me," six years ago, during the darkest days of his life. Its whispered refrain—"Alone, alive...Together, we're a lie"—was unforgettable, and paradoxically comforting. He soon became a diehard fan, purchasing everything the group released, immersing himself in the music, picking it apart, studying the lyrics, combing articles and blog posts for hints about the group's philosophy of music and intentions for each song. Psi-Kyll Soul was too off-the-wall for even the local college stations. He never forgot the review of one critic who described their second album as "amateurish electronic music with classical pretensions. A bizarre, brilliant, and beautiful worthless mess." All true, and that's what Robert loved about them. He converted Davin into a fan and, together, they tried to dissect everything they heard.

The group's unnamed musicians used a strange range as their primary instruments: violins, pianos, violas, xylophones, triangles, flutes, trumpets, banjos, various types of guitars, fiddles, pipe organs, synthesizers, harmoniums, and even theremins. Their old CD liner notes named neither the musicians nor the instruments, but Robert and Davin came up with their own list after repeated listening. Making their musical matters more interesting, the group also blended what they called "natural" sounds (dripping water, chirping crickets and birds, fighting squirrels, men coughing and laughing uncontrollably, women crying and having histrionic orgasms, children screaming and yawning, and fingers tapping, snapping, and cracking) with what they considered "unnatural" sounds (sirens, cowbells, whistles, starter pistols, breaking glass, slamming doors, rattling keys, and crashing vehicles). To Robert, the result was irritating and entrancing, discordant yet beautiful.

Sin Limite and Soleil, the two self-proclaimed "vice-vocalists" who sang on their earliest songs, delivered lyrics a mixed-minded critic had once described as a harsh harmonious clash of Low Metaphysical and High Postmodernist poetry. Robert didn't know about all that, but it did seem Sin Limite sang with a voice that seemed forever submerged under smoke, while Soleil's voice seemed to glide over high mists, each droplet a petite note produced by a lost fairy princess. An over-the-top conception, Robert knew, but it seemed perfect for the two divine ladies who produced some very haunting tunes.

When he wasn't careful, his conceptions went further: Each twisted strain of Psi-Kyll Soul's music crawled into his ears, found and entered his mind, unraveled and traveled the passageways like a tiny mutant centipede, detaching a segment at random intervals, allowing its appendages to hook somites in whatever crevices, crannies, and nooks it could, while its main body crawled and carried on, emitting poisons to permeate the entire brain.

Fuck the critics. Listening to enough of this sort of music, he believed, would provoke and encourage him to look for the unseen aspects of life, common wonders hidden just beyond the sights of common folks. Pushed to such a path, he might even discover the reasons behind seemingly senseless murders, and the secrets shrouding life after death. *Goddamn, I miss mom...*

It took him forty minutes to complete his calculus problems for Wednesday. He'd even gotten a head start on the problems he guessed would be assigned for Thursday's class. He wasn't tired, but something about the intellectual labor made him feel unclean. He needed a shower before starting on econ.

Robert stretched his arms and removed his sweatshirt on the

way to the bathroom. He tossed it and his T-shirt in the hamper before turning to the mirror to examine his muscle tone, as he always did. He didn't feel fit unless he looked fit—but his examination was all too brief. His skin's color distracted him.

His hands and face looked normal. But his chest, arms, and stomach were eggplant, purple-bluish.

Robert's lower jaw moved up and down, his mouth soundless, his eyes wide. Skeptical thoughts disbelieved while scared ones ran frantically down the corridors of memory trying to discover what might've brought this about. His doubts grew stronger when he focused and pinpointed tiny, cherry-red pimples all over his chest and shoulders; he breathed a punctuated sigh of relief seeing there were only a few on his stomach. This all had to be some sort of grotesque side effect of his acne medication, which he suddenly realized he'd forgotten to take today.

But he'd been on the medication for weeks, and there were other days when he'd forgotten or just didn't want to take it. He'd never experienced anything like this with his previous pills. Not in his junior high days when, desperate to get rid of acne in time to attend a party, he purposely overdosed. Not when he'd had colds and couldn't take his medication because it might interfere with whatever cold remedies he was trying. Not when, out of frustration, he'd mixed old pills with newly prescribed pills, thinking that was sure to kill the elusive source of acne that had plagued him for too damn long. But, then again, the pills he was on now were relatively new to the market. Missing a day might randomly mess you up.

He stared at the horrible display until convinced just looking would solve nothing. It'd be best to do what he'd come into the bathroom to do, take a pill as soon as possible, and consider giving the body cream another try.

He sat on the toilet lid. Methodically, he removed his socks, undid his belt, and stood again to remove his pants. He only looked down after removing his underwear, breathing relief there were no bumps or discolored patches in any crucial areas, just a couple of blemishes on his thighs.

He stepped into the shower and turned on the water. He had to wash himself with soap and his hands; a washcloth would irritate, even on the surfaces where there were no bumps or discoloration. It took longer, but whatever. A wash, a little more homework, and a good night's rest would help pull his body back to a state of normalcy.

But what the hell had pulled it away? If not his medication, was all this the result of sampling the horrible concoctions brought for the "potluck" portion of Brian's party? The result of eating from unsanitary silverware or trays at school that day? Or yesterday? Or some other day? Did something sting him, provoking an allergic response? When? *What?* He wasn't aware of any allergies or potential allergic responses. He'd lived in the same area for years; he'd been stung and bitten by all kinds of insects; he was familiar with all the grasses, weeds, and other plants in the region; and as far as he knew, he hadn't been exposed to anything new recently. So to what was his body reacting? His thoughts ran in circles. It just had to be in some way connected with his prescribed medications and him not following instructions.

He shut off the water, grabbed his towel and dried most of his body while standing in the shower. After stepping out onto the rug, he went in front of the mirror as he continued rubbing the towel across his hair; with each hair no more than half an inch long, it was as easy to dry as the rest of his body. His chest and arms were still in the same condition, but this time, the familiar sight was less horrifying.

He turned to leave, fastening the towel around his waist for the walk back to his room. Prompted by shadows seen out of the corner of his eye, he made the mistake of glancing back at the mirror. One by one, curly black hairs detached from his scalp and floated upward in a spiral motion before stopping to hover in midair.

He was going bald, and in the most absurd manner imaginable. An hour could've passed, or maybe ten minutes. Either way, it didn't stop until the top of his head was clean and shiny. The half-inch hairs then slowly descended, stopping to hover and spiral in front of his face.

The spectacle of free-floating helices transfixed Robert. He wasn't thinking of time, his tired muscles, or his nakedness. He wasn't thinking anything at all when something tickled his nose. He sneezed and opened his eyes to see each drop of spittle attaching itself to a hair, dying it upon impact to one of seven different colors.

The hairs then spun faster, whirling and twirling, each one moving toward another, forming for a brief instant what appeared to be double helices as they vibrated with increasing speed, appearing as fuzzy blurs. Robert blinked to focus, but the fuzzy spots amassed and, in one swift movement, ascended up to the bathroom's light. All he saw next was darkness beyond pitch black.

7

Robert had woken up from his blackout at midnight to find himself tucked safely in his bed. He didn't know whether he'd put himself there or his father had carried him from the bathroom. When he began to think about it, he fell back to sleep. Now, eleven hours later, he was spending part of his lunch hour standing outside one of the school's side entrances, engaged in what he'd intended to be a heart-to-heart conversation that led to reconciliation.

"But, baby, I—"

"And I told you to *please* stop calling me 'baby'!" Leigh's voice had sounded rough the entire time they'd been arguing, as if a nasty fit of coughing had rendered her hoarse. The area around her eyes—red and puffy even before she'd confronted Robert—added to his suspicion she was possibly sick or, more likely, had quit crying just a few moments before the confrontation began. She looked as if she could start again at any moment.

"I know you've told me," he said with a shrug. "But not recently, right?"

"It always applies, Rob."

"But you've never even told me why."

She pointed her finger at his face. "You never tell *me* anything. At least not lately."

He began to protest, but he lost his words seeing Leigh's nails were painted some bizarre shade of green and brown, appearing more fungal than fashionable.

"'Baby' implies that I'm a child," she said. "Intellectually and emotionally underdeveloped. It's insulting, not endearing. You know—you *should* know—I can't stand it when women fall all into themselves when some dumb brute calls them 'baby,' as if it's the highest compliment on the planet."

Dumb brute? Robert thought. *She can't be referring to me.* The reference used to be "honey" which, he vaguely recalled, was the preferable term of endearment for both of the lucky-stuck participants in a relationship. It was sweet, it was sticky, and it was able to alleviate certain illnesses if used properly. He couldn't recall either of them using the word *honey* in a while.

"The philosophy goes," she continued, "that we're born into a love-hate-fixation triangle, where the lines alternate, and the three angles are lust, trust, and *must*—meaning *duty*."

She stared directly at Robert's chin, a contrary and annoying habit she'd developed when speaking on subjects she felt above the heads of her listener.

"A baby enters the lives of the two people who together make up a 'couple,'" she said, "both of whom have, theoretically, invested one hundred percent of their love into each other. But with the newborn, some of that love is withdrawn by one from the other member of the couple and is invested in the little one. Attentions are split, divided. But if there is no newborn—as there *isn't* with us—the use of the term 'baby' must mean that there is a third presence, that *I'm* the third presence, and the main love, *your* main love, is elsewhere, closer to home."

"*What?*" Robert barely followed each step of her logic, but he knew exactly what she was getting at. "You're saying that I have another girlfriend, a *real* girlfriend somewhere else, and that you're just my fake one? My mistress?"

"Why else then, huh?" Leigh raised her voice just as the wind began to pick up. "Why else keep up all this mystery?"

"Because mystery's the essence of love?" He ventured a joke, but it was undercut when the wind managed to get past his coat and shirt, irritating the pimples underneath. He bristled as he unzipped his coat and scratched his left shoulder blade.

"Love is not lying," Leigh said. "It's not attending parties without me. It's not screwing around, in *any* sense of the phrase, in public, humiliating me."

"I haven't done any of that!" Robert scratched his chest rapidly as he spoke. "Except for that one party, but I'm—"

"Only human? Can't help it?"

"No—"

"So, you can help it, but choose not to?"

"No, I—"

"Don't choose? Are just chosen, and don't care?"

"Leigh..." She'd switched from philosopher mode to lawyer. Robert couldn't think of anything to say beyond her name, worrying that any other words might be used against him.

He realized the root of their relationship's problem. It had nothing to do with what he did or didn't do with her. It was all about listening. When was the last time they'd really listened to each other? Had they ever? He still remembered the first time she spoke to him, complimenting him, divulging her secret crush. He remembered the time, but what exactly had she said? What had he said in return? He only knew his response had brought a smile to her face, made her blush. She was red in the cheeks now, but nowhere close to smiling.

"I can't stand it anymore," Leigh said as the wind picked up again. "The secrets and lies..."

"*We* are a secret," Robert said, scratching his lower back. "*One* secret. There's nothing between us but love." Even he didn't believe that at the moment, but it just felt like the right thing to say. He felt maybe if he kept talking, tried listening harder to her, he might remember why they'd gotten close—or had tried to—in the first place. "Yeah, lies surround us, but they have to. You know they have to. Your parents. My parents—"

"Your *dad*."

As good as a steak knife to the chest. She was fighting mad, and apparently wanted him homicidal. But he wouldn't let her push him. He needed to stay calm and rational.

"Love, relationships," he said, "are hard work. But ours especially, of which no one around here would approve, is even harder. And I think—" He stopped short when the wind picked up with a shrieking gust. It seemed to carry thoughts deep from his subconscious: *Why even bother? She's not for you. Save the effort for someone truly compatible.* When the shrieking stopped, Leigh was quick to respond.

"I'll tell you what *I* think." She pointed her index and middle fingers at his face. Her fingernail polish so disgusted him, he forced himself to look in her eyes. "We've been working on nothing but a goofy joke—and everyone but me is laughing!"

As Leigh kept ranting, Robert's gaze lazily moved from her eyes to her lips. The winds had stopped—or his skin had finally become accustomed to their irritating gusts—or neither. It didn't matter. His complete attention now shifted back and forth, indecisively, between two poles of the senses: hearing, focused solely on Leigh's words, and seeing, focused only on her lips. He was uncertain whether something crazy was happening with him or with her.

When they touched, Leigh's lips gave off brilliant flashes of light that cut razor-straight through the clouds of her condensed breath. It was as if her face were a camera, her eyes the lenses, taking ephemeral pictures, peeling off and discarding the thin films layered on the surfaces of Robert's eyes. He blinked after each flash, attempting to correct his blurry vision, as his attention shifted back to the sense of hearing.

"We don't go out," Leigh said. "We can't meet anywhere at any time and have any privacy. This so-called 'relationship' is just so *stupid*!" Click. Another flash. "We never do anything anymore. At this point it seems like we're just hiding the relationship from ourselves. The secret's *too* safe."

"I'm sorry that you feel—" Robert stopped short when he noticed how gravelly his voice now sounded, how *fake* it sounded. He coughed as Leigh continued.

"Yeah, sorry for me. Not for anything you've done. It's that 'baby' shit again, in a different guise, just another part of it. Another piece"—another flash of light—"just like those fairy-tale myths that mist up the heads of the simple-minded. Women and men alike. As if women are all unfulfilled half-humans, sleep-walking through illusions, waiting for some frog to hop up and kiss us, making our dreams come true. Well, you're cold-blooded all right, but I'm already wide awake!"

She'd gone back to philosopher mode. Angry philosopher. Robert tried to keep his cool. "It seems you have a lot of pent-up hostility..." *and that it's all just now coming out at me.* He'd no choice but to leave the second half unspoken as he heard his voice becoming increasingly...froggish.

He considered Leigh's fairy-tale allusion. A frog kisses a seemingly drugged princess and there's a bright flash, smoke billows from somewhere, and one or the other—maybe both—emerge into a clearing to show off the transformation that's occurred; there's been a physical transformation but also an increase in consciousness, a greater awareness. Something was happening to Robert's consciousness. He was sensing a transformation in Leigh, or in himself. She was turning from companion to enemy. And deep down he was—

"Corrupted!"

Robert lost his thoughts as Leigh—who'd been talking while he'd been ruminating—reinserted herself.

"There's no *love* here, Rob." Her voice deepened to a tone of desperation. "I tried, maybe we both tried, but after all this time—"

Another flash of light as she spoke. Robert quickly looked away, then back.

"Maybe our original sin was definition," Leigh said. "We threw the words around like seeds, presuming we knew what they were and what would come from them. But, we should have held them, and examined them, appraised them like gemstones so we'd be sure of what we had. All I want from you now, at this moment, is a little truth and transparency. In remembrance of how this all began."

At the second syllable of the word "began," Robert saw another flash. But he didn't blink or turn away this time. He closed his eyes and swallowed hard. He realized that, during their lopsided argument, Leigh's language was weirdly shifting—from snappy insults and clichés, to the philosophical and poetic, and back again, like a pendulum. Yeah, she'd gone off on philosophic rants before, but it was rare. Now she was taking it further, packing a lot into one argument. Teachers, parents, other teenagers—no one in his world talked like she was talking.

But then, for the first time in a while, he was really making an effort to listen. He couldn't recall her ever really opening up to him before, except when discussing her fears about college and adulthood. From what he could remember, that's all from inside themselves they'd ever really shared—mutual fears about the future. They never dwelled too much on the present because it was all about secrets and hiding. But now he thought about the present. What was she to him at this moment? He again considered the fairy-tale allusion, her comment on "original sin," gemstones... That was it. She's too needy. Like a leech, bleeding him with growing and irresolvable needs, mostly for attention. He had needs, too. But now he felt her like a leech, on his neck, or *in* his neck, disturbing the flow of blood from heart to head, discoloring his skin...like a princess biting a plum with a tiny green worm in it.

Robert scratched his stomach and opened his eyes to find Leigh's red, puffy ones squinting into his, fingers on both hands pointing furiously at him, her lips moving rapidly as a barrage of pulsing lights shot through thick clouds of cold breath. The flashes hit his eyes without relief. She was apparently yelling at him, but he only heard snippets of what she was saying: "Meaning...love...you...what...I...you...mean... go...think..."

The conjunction of sounds and lights lulled Robert, pulling him from the present moment into an area of timelessness, a place where there were no scenes, only sensations. He heard music. Psi-Kyll Soul's song thumped and bumped against intangible walls while a muted voice echoed, "Alone, alive...Together, we're a lie...Untie me..."

"A *lie*?" Leigh's shout jerked him out of his neverwhere reverie and thrust him into here-and-now. "*Untie* you? Am I keeping you prisoner?"

Robert's lips moved as if he were stammering, but no sounds would come out.

"Fine—go free! Go fuck whoever you want! We're *done*." Leigh huffed past him, entering the school just as the bell rang to end their lunch hour and their fight. He stood still, bewildered.

He'd tried to listen, tried to concentrate, but—what the hell happened? He began to wonder if he could get it together in time for his matches tomorrow—then his attention snapped back to the present, and he found himself standing next to his locker, its door open.

"Hey, Rob!"

Dazed, he turned to see Colin waving and coming toward him from down the hall among a throng of other students transitioning between classes.

"Where were you at—" Before Colin could finish, a metalhead emerged from the throng, blindsiding him.

"Hey, *yo!*" the metalhead said as he pushed him. "Think I'm a piece of shit, huh?"

Colin quickly recovered from his stumble and moved to react, but another metalhead emerged, again blindsiding Colin, shoving him into two passing students.

"How 'bout me? Think I'm shit?"

The first metalhead was the lanky kid Colin had bumped on Tuesday. The second was a much stockier kid. Both shared similar grungy hairstyles and wore the same type of dirty denim jacket and jeans. Two other kids who looked and dressed the same accompanied them.

All too familiar with the routine of in-school fights, the other students in the hall had already formed a semicircle around the soon-to-be combatants. Unlike the usual occurrence, they didn't form a complete circle. An opening allowed Robert a clear view of the action and unimpeded entry into the fray if and when he chose to join. But he was still stunned, paralyzed from the bizarre experience he'd just had with Leigh. He was still trying to process just how he'd gotten from there, outside, to here by his locker. And now new information was pouring in, messing up the mental works. What was this happening just fifty feet in front of him?

Colin was a strong and highly skilled wrestler, but he was outnumbered by the dirty-fighting brawlers, two of whom were clearly bigger and maybe even stronger. The four surrounded him, making it impossible for Colin to see all of them at once or to defend himself on all sides. When he moved toward one, two others moved forward in his blind spots to try to push or trip him. Disadvantaged, Colin threw sloppy punches at them, a few times managing to clip a jacket-padded shoulder, but doing no damage. Within about a minute, he stopped punching and started grappling. The next metalhead who stepped up from behind to push him was surprised when Colin spun around, grabbed his arms, and threw him, slamming him on the floor. Colin got on top and choked him with both hands, digging his nails into the neck's skin, as the surrounding onlookers became even more unruly, many of them cheering Colin on. When the other three metalheads moved in, Colin returned to his feet to take another one or two down. But he was overwhelmed and pushed to the ground.

The processes working in Robert's mind finally brought him to a complete recognition of what was happening. He slammed his locker door and started to head in. Before he'd gone five steps, however, he noticed four others pushing themselves through the thick of the semicircle. Greg, Darren, Kenny, and loudmouth freshman heavyweight Shawn pushed guys, girls, backpacks, and anything else in their way as they made four straight paths to the center of the action.

Hillbilly Darren, the first to get in, came up behind the metalhead standing nearest to him. He went in quick and low, reaching both of his arms around the metalhead's waist, locking his hands near his navel. The surprised kid struggled to get free, but was instead lifted off the floor as Darren stood straight up and then slammed the kid as hard as he could on his shoulder. Darren turned him over, straddled him, and started hitting him in the face—with the fist sporting his class ring. Meanwhile, Shawn and Kenny made first contact with their targets.

Kenny's target saw him coming and stood straight to face him. Without hesitating, Kenny hit the kid in his chin. When the kid stumbled, Kenny snatched one of his legs and held it up in the air. The kid hopped on his free leg before Kenny kicked him twice in the kneecap and flung him to the ground. Instead of mimicking Darren, who'd already drawn plenty of blood from his hollering victim, Kenny stomped on the kid's arm, chest, and thigh—the last a misstep made when he aimed for the groin. He didn't let up until he planted his snakeskin boot square on his victim's stomach, causing the metalhead to yell at the top of his lungs and curl up into a fetal position. He kept screaming as Kenny kicked him in the back, shouting all the while. "White trash dirtdog piece of shit! I'll kick your goddamn spine into pieces!"

Big Shawn acted as a bulldozer as he made contact with his target, lifted him a few inches off the ground, and push-carried the kid through the crowd of spectators, most of whom were smart enough to get out of the way. He picked up speed as he moved, stopping only when his struggling victim's back hit a brick wall and the back of his head cracked the glass door of a fire extinguisher case. The metalhead screamed as Shawn let go of his waist only to grab the kid's face with his right hand and shatter the glass completely by shoving the back of his head into the case's door. He let his crying victim fall before he started punching him in his kidneys.

Greg had gone straight for the metalhead who had Colin's arm pinned down under his knee. He shoved him off of Colin and, before the metalhead could react, hit him in the ear and in the neck. The kid stayed on his knees, sheltering his head with his arms as he screamed. Greg scrambled to help Colin as he sat up and tried to get to his feet. "You okay, man?"

"These assholes..." Colin rubbed his arm.

"You okay?" Greg repeated. "Anything serious?"

"Don't think so," Colin said. He then winced when he touched his lip and found blood on his fingertips. "These bastards..." Colin shook his arm to bring back the normal flow of circulation as Greg looked at it.

"Nothin's broken, right?"

"Naw...*shit*..." Colin grunted as Greg helped him stand.

"Here, go see Coach Sanders," Greg said, referring to the assistant wrestling coach who administered first aid at meets. "We'll send these dirtdogs back to their shit-spots in the base-ment." He then turned to kick his crouching victim in the face. He missed, but seemed to think nothing of it as he lunged and landed on top of him, hammering his fists as fast as he could on whatever part of the metalhead's body caught his eye.

Colin stared as Greg punched and cursed. He seemed to be contemplating whether he should join in and take revenge, or simply take Greg's advice. He apparently chose the latter as he turned away, briefly meeting Robert's eyes. In that moment, Robert thought he saw a scowl twisting on Colin's face.

The screaming and swearing and cheering grew even louder and harder on the ears when several teachers came running down different halls. They fought their way through the crowd—with considerably more trouble than the wrestlers had—and tried to pull the boys away from their bawling, bleeding victims. They called for everyone to "Break it up!" and "Stop it!" and for other adults within earshot to come back them up. The school's security officers were nowhere in sight—or even in earshot, it seemed—but within minutes, seven teachers appeared on the scene restraining the boys and preparing to march them to the principal's office.

Robert remained rooted, staring at the crowd that had suddenly become deathly silent. In his eyes, the whole scene gradually bathed itself in a pale watery light. All colors faded and slid to the periphery before leaving his view altogether. As if with the aid of some alien consciousness within him, he deduced he'd just witnessed a clip from a motion picture, something from a larger film project, something made by connecting strips of film that had been peeled from the surfaces of other eyes, a multitude, none of them his own.

Before he could retake control of the part of his mind temporarily stolen from him in order to form the questions and seek the answers, he came back to his common senses, forgot the alien presence, and found himself sitting in his next class, with his hand raised.

8

Darren, Colin, and Greg stood in their underwear, looking on. Another boy, wearing only a jock strap, stepped up onto the scale. Robert didn't care to look.

The boy and other wrestlers in line to be weighed and examined by the officials were all under 275 pounds. They were all either completely naked or close to it—nothing nice to look at. Robert instead gazed at the teammates who'd been involved in yesterday's brawl. None of them showed any emotion. It was exactly what Coach Myers demanded during weigh-ins. His wrestlers stood straight-backed, stone-faced, and in the buff to show off the chiseled physiques they worked year-round to maintain—all part of the strategy to psych out opponents.

The three brawlers' expressionless faces were also having an effect on Robert's psyche. The hillbilly, the black boy, and the redneck. White, black, and red. He wondered what they were thinking. What had they thought about their actions yesterday? And what did they think of Robert's hesitation and ultimate failure to join in?

He hadn't spoken to any of them in more than twenty-four

hours, but he'd heard of the fight's aftermath. Two of the metal-heads went to the emergency room. The parents of the other two picked them up and undoubtedly took them to the ER as well. Darren, Kenny, Greg, and Shawn all spent one period in the principal's office and were each given a choice of either going home for the remainder of the day or returning to their classes. All four chose class, probably because it would've been a hassle to have to go all the way home just to turn around and come all the way back to attend Coach Myers's pretournament pep talk after school. Attendance for all wrestlers was mandatory.

Double standards indeed, Robert thought, though he was glad his teammates were at the tournament, in good health, and ready to wrestle. And he felt little pity for the metalheads' pain and suffering. They'd gotten just what they'd deserved. It was, however, a little disturbing that absolutely no one was punished or even threatened with suspension. Robert wondered if he were alone in thinking there'd been no need for his teammates' excessive brutality. Darren, Kenny, Greg, and Shawn were wrestlers. *Grapplers.* Surely they could've gotten the metalheads off Colin without punching or kicking, and pinned them down until adults arrived. Maybe the principal and some of his administrative colleagues were bigger wrestling fans than anyone knew. Or maybe they were just wise and cowardly, hoping to avoid pissing off the coaches and the team's redneck fans by withdrawing half the wrestlers from the most important wrestling meet so far this season.

All six wrestlers from Robert's high school had weighed in at least two pounds below their allowed weight limit. They'd also been examined for facial hair, lengthy fingernails, and any cuts or scratches that could become potential problems during a match. Robert was shocked when he stepped on the scale and saw he weighed 149 pounds, ten lighter than he expected. His nervousness multiplied when the officials took what seemed to be an extra amount of time examining his back. They whispered to one another and grumbled while Coach Myers stood off to the side, glaring. But they finally said nothing other than Robert was okay to wrestle.

He'd sighed, thankful he hadn't been seeing things when he examined his own back in the mirror that morning. Except for the old wrestling-related scars and bruises, his skin was completely free of the eggplant tint and cherry-red pimples of just a day ago. His idea of tripling up his acne medication and using the body cream on Wednesday morning had been a risky one, and probably—he hoped—been responsible for the itching and hallucinations he'd experienced throughout the day, particularly when arguing with Leigh. But from the moment he left his bed this morning, he'd felt fine. He was alert and clearheaded, nearly clear-skinned and feeling energetic, ready to wrestle.

It was nearing eight p.m. Every wrestler from every team had made weight. When the other wrestlers, clothed, left the area for their respective preparation rooms, Coach Myers finally allowed Robert and his teammates to get dressed in their street clothes. The coach then walked over to speak to some of the officials and other coaches while Assistant Coach Sanders stayed with the boys.

"You guys feeling okay?" Coach Sanders was ostensibly speaking to all of them, but Robert could tell by his tone and gaze that he meant Colin, Darren, and Greg.

"Yep."

"Yeah."

"Ready to go."

"Good," Coach Sanders said, his face as expressionless as theirs. "Because you all have tough opponents for your first matches, particularly Colin and Greg. Rob, your guy's not as hot as some think; we've been studying him closely for much of his high school career, but he's been known to pull off some miracles for some quick unexpected wins."

"I've faced him before," Robert said as he fastened his belt.

"But not at this level. He coasts during regular season matches, against opponents he doesn't seem to respect. But in tournaments, that's where he really shines. Be alert. Don't give up anything."

"I'm ready," Robert said, wondering just what sort of miracles Bruce Webster, his barely above-average opponent, was known to perform. They'd faced each other on four previous occasions, going all the way back to junior high. Robert had beaten him twice, and only narrowly missed winning a third time. He'd also seen Bruce wrestle others, in person and on tape. While he didn't study him like his coaches did, he never saw Bruce execute anything approaching a stunning or miraculous move. He'd only seen lucky wins, mostly due to Bruce's out-of-shape opponents reaching a state of exhaustion in less than five minutes. Bruce had only made it to tournament levels in the past due to poor competition in his weight class. And even though Bruce had dropped a few pounds this season to move down to a new class, Robert still wasn't surprised to see that he'd advanced so far again. His weight class was tough and competitive, but not nearly as much as Colin's or Darren's. Robert had prepared mentally for this tournament by swearing out loud that he'd do well. Now he silently vowed to make a name for himself during the first match by embarrassing Bruce.

He stood up from tying his shoes as Coach Myers passed by. "C'mon!"

Colin, Darren, Matthew, Robert, Rusty, Greg, and Coach Sanders all followed him to the team's preparation room. They'd put on their wrestling singlets and warm-up suits, perform some warm-up exercises, and listen to fiery encouragement speeches from the coaches. Robert only needed to change into his wrestling attire. He was sufficiently fired up already.

∽

THE TEAM SAT in a semicircle around Coach Myers. Coach Sanders stood behind them. All were fully engrossed, or at least pretending to be. Coach Myers's encouragement speeches were all generally the same in content and purpose. Often they were barely coherent. Today, it made sense to Robert, and he was with the coach all the way as he wound up.

"Now is *not* the time to shine by lettin' your giddiness about gettin' here get the better of you, make you make stupid mistakes, *lose* yourself out there on the mat," Coach Myers said. "Keep your eyes on that summit! Don't quit, damn it! Whenever you get tired, if you feel like restin', stoppin' for a minute, repeat to yourself: Don't quit, damn it! That's your motto! Repeat it to yourself silently, over and over and over from now until you step on that mat so it'll stay in your mind, it'll come to you automatically, every few seconds, as those six minutes tick away. No time for coastin', no time for restin'. Go all out—explode! Give it your all and don't let up, right? But don't be *stupid* either. Wrestle smart, wrestle hard, wrestle with *heart*! Now let's close our eyes and have a little silence, think about what's gotta be done, and about the ones who couldn't be here tonight."

As everyone bowed their heads, Robert wondered if Coach Myers's last sentence was intended to be a signal they should remember Davin, in sadness, and *hope* for him to recover from whatever affliction he had...or was it a veiled desire for him to get worse, deserved payback for ducking out and away from the team when they needed him most? Robert banished both thoughts from his mind, not wanting to let his suspicions get the best of him. Coach Myers was right. There was work to do this night, and the next two days. Right now there was only one thing to think about. In remembrance of his mother: *Don't quit, damn it...Don't quit, damn it...Don't quit, damn it...*

ON THE SURFACE, Allan High School's main gymnasium was located in a building separate and distinct from the school building, but a narrow underground tunnel used in emergency situations actually connected the two buildings. The gymnasium's separateness and size made it an ideal location for the regional wrestling tournament; it had undoubtedly been prepared for the three-day competition without disturbing classes and other academic activities. Black wrestling mats with yellow markings covered most of the gymnasium's floor. Three big yellow circles permitted three wrestling matches to take place simultaneously.

Two rounds of wrestling for every weight class would take place on Thursday night; a full day of wrestling would take place on Friday; and the final rounds and awards ceremony would take place on Saturday. Those who finished in the top four in each weight class would advance to the state finals tournament to be held on the Friday and Saturday of the following week. Robert's seventeenth birthday was on that Friday. He intended to celebrate it in style.

The Howard Phillips High School Warriors had seven wrestlers qualify for the regional tournament, but due to Davin's absence, they'd have to forfeit their spot in the 112-pound weight class. Still, six was better than none. Many other schools' teams had only one or two wrestlers representing them at the meet. Two teams, both regarded as the best in the region, had nine wrestlers. Hundreds of audience members had traveled long distances for the sole purpose of seeing which of those two would win the tournament. Many had taken off work or skipped school in order to get good seats.

There was no need for Robert or his teammates to skip any part of the school day for travel. Weigh-ins had begun at six p.m. Howard Phillips High had let out just before three-thirty. It was a little more than an hour's drive between the two schools, and there was little to no rush-hour traffic on the route. Nonetheless, the Warrior coaches insisted on arriving early to get settled into their motel rooms, check their wrestlers' weights before the official weigh-ins, and go through one quick and easy practice session in their private preparation room.

When they were ready, Robert's coaches (dressed in black suits and red-and-blue ties) and his teammates (wearing their all-black warm-up suits and carrying their headgear in their hands), filed out of their room and walked to their designated area at the side of the gym floor. After the national anthem and other minor opening ceremony activities, the battles of strength and will and heart were set to begin.

ROBERT AND BRUCE stood in the center of the circle, their shoulders hunched, staring icicles at each other.

"Shake hands," the referee said.

They quickly and firmly shook once and then returned to their wrestling stances. The whistle blew. Robert and Bruce both shot in for a takedown without even bothering to set up their attacks. Robert's shot, however, was a trick.

He'd lunged in and snapped back, returning to his stance as Bruce followed through, reaching for Robert's left ankle to execute a low single-leg takedown. Robert got his legs back and away from Bruce. He tapped the top of Bruce's head to both misdirect attention and post himself as he spun around, grabbed an arm and an ankle, and exerted pressure forward, forcing Bruce flat onto his stomach.

"Takedown! Two points!"

Bruce grunted while Robert jammed his forearm against the left side of Bruce's face as he grabbed Bruce's right shoulder. As Robert applied more pressure with his arm, Bruce struggled to turn his face to the left; he was trying to stand up.

Robert touched Bruce's right knee to make it seem like he was going for the pinning combination known as a "cradle." But as Bruce struggled with his limited freedom to counter it, Robert quickly released his cross-face hold and wrapped both of his arms around Bruce's left leg. Bruce got on his hands and one knee, one position further in his quest to stand up.

Outside the circle, in one corner of the mat, Bruce's coach shouted at him. In the opposite corner, Coach Myers was also shouting, but Robert heard nothing more than a dull roar, a gray snowy noise—like an aural reflection of the referee's black-and-white uniform. He was in his own zone, determined to pin Bruce in the first period, giving him the ultimate humiliation.

Bruce twisted and jerked through every movement his limited range of freedom allowed, but Robert's grip was too tight. Without the full control of both legs, it was impossible for Bruce to stand up. Undoubtedly realizing this, he decided on a craftier move: flee in order to fight. He tried to use his hands and free knee to crawl out of the circle so that the referee would pause the match and Robert would release his hold. They'd have to resume the match in referee's position, with Bruce on his hands and knees, and Robert on top and behind him, still in control, but with much less than he had now.

But Bruce's plan went nowhere. Every time he moved a few inches forward, Robert inched backward on his knees, bringing Bruce with him.

Bruce switched tactics again, from fleeing to fighting, mostly by trying to twist his leg and force it free by kicking at Robert. This also was futile as Robert adjusted his grip so all Bruce could do was squirm his left foot. His right foot, however, was free, and in an inspired wild attempt to scramble away from Robert, it kicked him in his right knee.

There was pain upon impact, almost too small for any reaction, but Robert winced. His eyes didn't close completely; he simply squinted. When they opened wider, however, he saw silver glitter where the shoe had hit.

What the hell did Bruce step in? he thought before noticing the silver specks weren't just on his knee but sprinkled all over his right leg. And all over his left leg. A tiny piece of sparkling silver was lodged in every third or fourth hair follicle.

Robert expected to find the glitter on Bruce's leg as well, but he saw nothing but a thin film of sweat. On Robert's skin, it seemed the silver was spreading. His arms, his wrists, his hands —silver specks rested in random hair follicles and the crevices of the hairless patches.

He was on the verge of losing his concentration, on the edge of losing his grip, on the way perhaps to losing the match. He realized all of this a moment before a few of the high school and local newspaper photographers near the edge of the mat took several pictures in rapid succession. The silver dust on his skin seemed to absorb the cameras' flashing lights as they hit. Patches of his skin shifted from brown to a deep dark green.

Before Robert could even take a breath, time in his mind shifted, and an alien presence entered the center of his consciousness.

He stood straight up, still holding Bruce's leg. A shocked and off-balance Bruce planted his hands and free foot, looking like an arching bridge as the rest of his body was up off the mat.

Without a thought, Robert released his hold and shot his body straight underneath the bridge. On the way, his right arm grabbed Bruce's right leg while his left arm grabbed Bruce's right triceps, sweeping Bruce's right arm out from under him. Bruce collapsed onto Robert's head and shoulders, but Robert kept driving forward until his head caught in the mat. He stood on his pate and flipped over Bruce's body as it rolled on the mat.

Robert tilted Bruce on his left side and, having trapped and locked Bruce's right arm and leg with his arms, sat with his back braced against Bruce's chest and stomach. As Robert applied pressure backward, Bruce tried to use his free arm for a countermove. But before Bruce could even touch him, Robert let go of the leg, rolled to his left, and swept Bruce's head with his right arm, locking his hands under Bruce's left shoulder and squeezing with almost all his strength while using the rest to apply pressure with his chest.

With his head and left arm locked in Robert's hold, Bruce's shoulders were nearly flat, and he couldn't budge them. The referee's hand smacked the mat. Bruce was pinned.

Robert released his hold, sprang to his feet, and ran to the center of the circle. His teammates and some in the audience appeared to be cheering. Robert didn't hear a thing.

Bruce was still in the spot where he'd lost, resting on a knee. He was looking down at the mat, breathing heavily, almost heaving. His coaches were on their feet, furious and yelling. Robert saw, but still heard nothing. They were screaming either at Robert or at the referee, or at both. They kept pointing at Robert and the area on the mat where he'd scored his victory. All the pointing made Robert increasingly self-conscious, bringing him completely back to the here-and-now.

He knew he'd just won, and he knew he'd won by pinning his opponent, but he wasn't exactly sure how he'd done it. The last thing he clearly remembered was silver dust and a change in skin color. He quickly checked himself over—all of the exposed skin, his shoes, his wrestling singlet. Everything looked normal. The dust had apparently rubbed off.

Robert shivered as waves of chilliness overtook him. He looked over to the slowly rising Bruce, wishing he'd hurry up, come over, and shake hands so that he could get off the mat and cover up. The referee was also impatient, motioning for Bruce to quicken his pace as he shuffled toward the circle.

Robert took off his headgear. The first clear sounds he heard were from Bruce's coaches: "...kind of garbage is *this*? He was *choking* him!" "*Illegal* moves, ref! At least *two* of them!" The referee appeared to ignore them as he again motioned for Bruce to hurry up so he and Robert could shake hands, officially ending the match.

After they finally shook and released, the referee raised Robert's hand, and both wrestlers turned to walk off of the mat. Bruce's coaches rushed forward to argue with the referee at close range. Robert walked toward the corner where his coaches were standing. Silent. Scowling.

"What the hell was that, Goldner?" Coach Myers asked.

"What was what?" Robert said, still trying to catch his breath. "I won."

"What the hell were you *doing*?" Coach Sanders asked. "Do you know what you looked like out there?"

Robert didn't answer, thinking of his brief skin color change.

"All that wild crazy bullshit," Coach Sanders said, "standing on your head, flipping over. We don't teach that in practice. You could've hurt yourself, and your opponent! What you were doing was borderline illegal!"

The two coaches for Bruce's team were still arguing with the referee and another official who'd joined him. The matches on the other mats continued.

"I told you to show some heart tonight," Coach Myers said. "I didn't think I'd have to tell you—*you*, of all people—to show some intelligence! As long as you wrestle for Howard Phillips, you do *only* the moves we teach in practice, understand?"

"Yes," Robert said, "but my skin—"

"Go dry off and get your warm-up suit on before you catch a cold. We can't have you getting sick before tomorrow."

But after tomorrow would apparently be fine with him, Robert thought. He'd no control over what happened to him during the brief moments before his win. He didn't even have a clear memory of it. He wasn't sure he could prevent it from happening again. But what did it matter if it meant a win in the end? Who on his team would cry about that?

As he got into his warm-up garments, he saw the coaches for Bruce's team had either resolved their dispute or given up their argument with the officials. They'd gone to monitor a match involving one of their wrestlers on another mat. On Robert's team, only Greg had yet to wrestle before the first round was over. Every other wrestler on the team, including Colin, had won their matches. But since Darren and Robert were the only two who'd managed to pin their opponents, Robert felt he deserved at least a little bit of praise from his coaches. After all, it was a win for them, too. And no one harassed Darren when it seemed like he was trying to dislocate his opponent's shoulder. The other wrestler's coaches didn't even whimper in protest.

He'd only get his coaches' respect by going through and winning the whole damn tournament in his weight class. For now at least his teammates congratulated him on his incredible match.

"Now in the next round, let's see you make your guy cry and *give up* in the first period!" Darren chuckled while slapping Robert on the back.

"Yeah, make him want to quit his team and go home right after you shake his hand," Rusty laughed.

Greg was the only one who didn't participate in the round of accolades. He remained off to the side, down on one knee with his face buried in one hand. It was his way of getting mentally prepared for his match. A kind of prebattle prayer stance— maybe directed to an outer deity, or maybe to some inner fighting spirit. Or possibly to both. Robert gazed at him. The smile that had spread across his face as his teammates praised him disappeared.

Greg was at the end of the Warriors' lineup for tonight. Davin was supposed to be at the beginning. Robert considered going off to the side for some prayer time of his own. A look inward could help him keep in mind that certain spirits were around him, surrounding him—the spirits of those who were currently in sickness and those who'd passed too soon. He couldn't forget he wasn't out to succeed for his own glory or honor, or even for the reputation of the team. For his next match, and all those to come after it, with this remembrance, Robert would follow the admonition his father had once given him, and step onto the mat with a fire in his eyes.

GREG LOST BY ONE POINT. As the seconds of the match's third and final period ticked away, it seemed as if he might succeed in scoring a takedown and gaining a couple of points on his opponent. But Greg was fatigued. His opponent was just as fatigued, but the guy was also a point ahead; he could afford to coast, concentrating solely on defending himself while he maintained his lead. Trying to maneuver a takedown, Greg had too much to think about and not enough time.

There was a fifteen-minute break between the tournament's first and second rounds. Robert's coaches said little to the Warriors as they stretched and loosened their limbs and gave each other words of encouragement. The coaches used the time to study each team's standings after the wins and losses of the first round.

"Awright, men, let's go out," Coach Myers said ten minutes into the break. "We can still win this." The Warriors, decked out in their warm-up attire, filed out of their preparation room with their coaches right behind.

Halfway into it, round two's match results yielded no surprises. In the 125-pound weight class, Matthew beat his opponent by six points. In the 130-pound weight class, Colin lost, but was not pinned. At 145 pounds and 152 pounds, Darren and Rusty, respectively, won their matches, though neither was able to pin his opponent. It was now time for Robert to humiliate his opponent in the 160-pound weight class.

"Let's go, Goldner," Coach Sanders said as he clapped his hands. "Mat number three. Strike quick. Flick this fish to his back."

"Yeah, fry this bastard!" Rusty said.

Robert removed his right hand from his face and rose up off of his knee. On his feet, he bounced from foot to foot, lightly jogging in place as he whispered the remainder of his encouraging poem, part invocation.

"C'mon Rob, do it!"

"Do it *again!*"

Other teammates clapped and encouraged him, even Colin, who was most likely fighting the crushing depression he felt after losing. Robert and Coach Sanders jogged to the corner edge of mat number three, where Coach Myers was already sitting.

"Let's go, Goldner," Coach Myers said. "Put some fire in those eyes."

Robert removed his warm-up jacket and pants. As he tossed them aside, pinpricks burned on his arms and legs. He sucked a breath through clenched teeth, scrunching his placid expression into a grimace.

"That's it, Goldner!" Coach Sanders said. "Put your match face on! Go to it!"

Robert hustled to the center of the circle, examining himself on the way. He saw nothing unusual, but he still felt the burning pinpricks. It didn't help that the air he sucked through his teeth made a sizzling sound.

He assumed his stance in the circle's center and looked his opponent in his unblinking eyes: Cole Bishop, ranked Virginia's third-best high school wrestler in the 160-pound weight class. He had only two losses for the current season, three fewer than Robert.

"Shake hands."

Robert's and Cole's palms slapped and slid apart. The referee's whistle shrieked. The sound easily passed the padded coverings of Robert's headgear, glided through his ear canals at twice the speed, and stabbed through his brain, flash-throbbing at his temporal lobe.

He fell down to a knee, effectively countering a headlock throw Cole had tried to execute, but he was back on his feet in a second, circling with Cole, who repeatedly reached for his wrists and neck to set up some other takedown.

Robert grimaced and even growled, not only feeling the acid in his skin's pores, but also hearing the whistle's ghost jabbing at his gray matter.

Cole attempted to pick his ankle, but Robert blocked. He faked his own ankle pick as a setup for a reverse headlock, but Cole evaded. The coaches of both yelled encouragement from the corners.

Cole's face had the serene expression Robert liked to display when trying to psych out opponents who were physically stronger but mentally weaker. *Make your opponent think you're too good to care what they do; you're skillful enough to counter and win anyway, without losing a single bead of sweat.* Robert couldn't control the way his face appeared, and he didn't try. He struggled instead to get control of one or both of Cole's wrists while trying to prevent him from getting close enough to tie up with him, ear-to-ear or forehead-to-ear. Cole could easily overpower him while they were on their feet. His only option was to take Cole down and control the match from surprising beginning to victorious end.

They circled for a few seconds more, both of them snatching at the other's hands, wrists, or elbows. Then in a blink, Cole stood up straight and dove down bind in to execute a double-leg take-down. Even though it was a common setup and rarely worked on an alert wrestler, the stand-up trick fooled Robert into mimicking. His standing up gave Cole his opening.

Robert sprawled, getting his legs back and away, and applied pressure with his upper body to Cole's back, but Cole held on to

Robert's legs and drove forward on his knees. With one hand on the back of Cole's head, Robert tried to push it down into the mat while his other hand tried to pry one of Cole's hands off his leg, giving him the mobility to spin around on Cole's back and get behind him.

Cole kept applying pressure forward and upward while trying to force Robert to the mat. Robert exerted himself as much as he could—but he ultimately failed and found himself lying on his stomach and elbows.

"Two! Takedown!" the referee shouted.

"—up, Goldner, up!" Coach Sanders yelled.

He didn't need instruction. Upon impact, Robert scrambled to his knees and tried to get to a standing position, but Cole had a firm grasp on Robert's right ankle and an arm wrapped around his waist. Robert realized his loss of control, panicked, and did what he could to get his other leg out of Cole's reach.

Robert placed his hand on the arm at his waist to prevent it from stopping him as he sat up halfway and thrust his free leg out in front of him. He was now in an uncomfortable if not painful splits position, with Cole pulling his right ankle far behind him, and his left leg thrust out-of-reach in front.

"*Careful*, Goldner!" Coach Sanders shouted.

"Keep wrestling!" Cole's coach shouted. "Keep wrestling!"

Cole held on to Robert's ankle and applied more pressure forward, forcing Robert's nose closer and closer toward his outstretched leg's knee. Robert was flexible enough to withstand the awkward positioning, grunting just a little as he applied counterpressure backward. He squinted, but his eyes didn't close. His face was close enough to his leg to see thin lines in the skin. He relented in his backward counterpressure to Cole's weight, allowing himself to be pushed closer to his leg as his eyes narrowed into a tighter squint. There were many fine lines, all of them black, like strands of hair embedded in his skin—but as he stared, they shifted, curved, became circles, ovals, linked...into chains. He held his breath as the chains' circuitous pattern became luminous, emitting a faint green glow.

"*Watch* yourself, Goldner!" Coach Myers yelled. "Be careful!"

He realized too late that his face was too close to his leg. He'd allowed Cole too much. Cole released Robert's ankle, draped an arm over Robert's neck, and threaded his other arm under the knee of Robert's outstretched leg. Cole's hands touched and locked. He had Robert in a tight, inescapable cradle.

"*Shhh...*" Robert breathed through clenched teeth as Cole rolled him to his back—

"Time!" the referee yelled after tweeting his whistle.

Cole immediately released his hold and ran back to the center of the mat. He showed no frustration that he'd been only a second away from victory, but he was clearly eager to finish the job.

Robert took his time returning to the circle's center, trying to stretch and loosen his legs as he walked. He looked down as he straightened his headgear and saw no evidence of lines or patterns, black or green. Knowing the score was 2–0 in Cole's favor, he got down in referee's position, on his hands and knees, when he reached the center of the circle.

"You're down four points, Goldner," Coach Myers yelled, "with only four minutes left in the match!"

Damn. He'd given up two additional points to Cole for almost going to his back.

"Strike it up here!" Coach Sanders called. "No time to coast!"

Cole put his hands together, forming a diamond shape, and showed it to the referee.

"He's letting you go, Rob!" Coach Sanders yelled. "You know what to do!"

Yeah, come halfway up, faking a stand-up, but instead reverse to snatch the guy's legs or ankles. Easier thought than accomplished. The maneuver only worked against wrestlers who had less competence than Cole. But Robert needed to find some way to catch his opponent off guard. The only win he could get in this match would be by way of a few surprise moves.

Cole placed his hands between Robert's shoulder blades. Robert heard the abbreviated cheers and remarks of his teammates sitting at the edge of the gym floor. Then the whistle blew. Its echoing shrieks skittered through Robert's ears and around his mind as he crawled forward, unencumbered.

Cole had undoubtedly expected him to try to stand up; the crawling probably confused him. He scurried to catch up, but Robert abruptly stopped, came up to a knee, and turned to face him. Cole stopped too late. He was too close when Robert lunged and just barely grasped one of his ankles. Cole tried to sprawl but couldn't with his right ankle captured and being pulled to Robert's chest.

Robert worked his way up Cole's wriggling leg and Cole ended up in a crescent shape, his free leg thrust back while his upper body leaned over onto Robert, clearly determined to take him down.

Robert applied pressure to Cole's leg with his upper body, but Cole managed to stand. Robert stood with him, keeping the leg pressed tightly against his chest.

"You got 'im, Rob!"

"Take him down! Take him back down!"

Cole hadn't escaped yet. Robert was still in an ideal position to execute a single-leg takedown. No doubt realizing this, Cole hopped frantically, struggling to get free.

By this time, several newspaper photographers had gathered around the mat. Knowing he was in a prime position, Robert decided to relinquish some control to instinct. *Let anxious reason rest; let the years of training take over.* He still heard the referee-whistle's scratchy whispers in his head and hoped that if he willingly loosened the rational grasp of his mind, it would lessen their impact.

He loosened his grip on Cole's leg and let his Warrior instinct prepare the takedown. Nearby, cameras flashed in rapid succession. Bursts of blue assaulted Robert's eyes before a red-tinged blackness overcame his vision. The mewling whispers in his mind swelled to a massive spiked ball of cacophonous sound, replacing his gray matter, occupying his skull, scraping the bone from the inside as it turned, revolving at nearly the speed of light.

Robert screamed his throat dry. Flames kissed and licked his skin. He released his hold and Cole briefly returned to his wrestling stance before moving in.

Nearly blind but sensing a fast-approaching enemy, Robert quickly and *firmly* grabbed Cole's crotch while his other hand snatched and pinched his shoulder, effectively numbing his right arm.

Cole screamed when grabbed, but cut it short when pinched. He sputtered curses but they were mostly buried under the mingling sounds of the referee's incessant whistle-blowing, coaches stomping and protesting, and audience members roaring at the sight of Robert lifting Cole over his head and tossing him.

He landed several feet away, hitting the mat's edge on his left arm and shoulder. Cole cried out as he rolled onto the hard gym floor. First aid personnel and Cole's coaches ran to assist him; the referee signaled to the scorekeepers that Robert was disqualified; and Robert's own coaches and others rushed to restrain him.

The first two people to reach him recoiled when Robert looked as if he was about to attack them. Convulsions shook him like a rag doll and continued even after he collapsed on the mat. A minute passed before someone recognized that a seizure was contorting Robert's body into circus-freakish positions. Someone called for first aid personnel to rush over with equipment.

Robert saw and heard everything through a cloud of smoke. His body felt entangled in a briar patch, the thorny vines growing out from inside his own mind, each prickly thorn a match that sparked and lit up when it brushed against his ripped, burning flesh. He couldn't stop screaming as the vines ensnarled him, growing and growing, feeding on the fire and darkness, the pain and noise.

He was trapped in a loop. He was trapped in barbed chains...

The vines drew him back into his mind as they packed his soul into the cacophonous spiked ball that rolled and scraped and chipped away at his skull until it was nothing but bone fragments and his own head could no longer contain him.

PART II

———

DERANGED

1

—————

It was Saturday morning when Robert found he'd been disqualified from his match and ejected from the tournament for intentionally trying to injure his opponent. He'd experienced an epileptic seizure during his final match on Thursday, bleeding all over the mat by scratching himself as if trying to peel his skin off. After he blacked out, he slept—first on the mat, then in a hospital bed—for more than twenty-four hours.

By Saturday morning, his cuts, bruises, and scratches had mostly—miraculously—disappeared. He'd stabilized enough to be released into the care of his father, who had met Coach Sanders at one hospital on Thursday night, just hours before he was transferred to a different facility. Midday Saturday, his father drove him home, fed him tomato soup and toast, and put him straight to bed.

On Sunday morning, he had no fever. He didn't sweat and his eyes looked fine. No nausea, no headache, no ringing in the ears, no dizziness. He wasn't ravenous at breakfast, nor did he pick at his food. His father took all of this into account before deeming him healthy enough to attend church, a place that could only help to make him healthier. Robert had said next to nothing since waking up. It was only in the car that he began to stutter, as if his whole body was again under attack.

"I-I-I...I...I...I..."

"*Easy*, Robert," his father said. "Just relax."

It wasn't easy. Not with the mind-bending, thought-breaking sounds of Sun Ra's Arkestra coming out of the car's speakers for the entire ride. His father had once described this music as that which had traveled backward in time, descending purely from the high future—where it sounded perfect—only to arrive in the present-day as something malformed, unstructured, and abstract. Beautiful concept, but it just contributed to his ugly feeling this morning.

He didn't know how the tournament had ended nor how his teammates had fared, nor did he give a shit anymore. All he knew was that, by being disqualified, by being unable to advance to the state wrestling tournament, by being denied the opportunity to win it, he remained damned. A damned mistake.

His mother had died six years ago, on his birthday. Died... Hell, she'd been *murdered*. While out gathering his presents, she was slaughtered like an animal, cut up by her no-good druggie cousin. This year, Robert's birthday fell on the first day of the state wrestling tournament. Winning it all was to be less a celebration for him than a tribute to her. She'd cared less for sports than his father did, but to achieve something spectacular in an activity respected in the eyes of many—especially many racist rednecks—he believed this feat would be felt by her, wherever her soul was now. His achievement would perhaps add some prideful warmth to a soul undoubtedly chilled by the experience of an early death.

His mother was highly religious in her time on Earth. Robert considered himself a one-foot-out-of-the-closet skeptic, distrustful of organized religion and those who constantly touted their "spirituality," while his father viewed the church more as an organizing tool for the black community than a place to worship what he considered a careless if not brazenly malevolent creator-god. Nevertheless they both regularly attended Rev. Herbert Richardson's church. The reverend was another of his mother's cousins. A drug- and drama-free one. Robert hoped his attendance this Sunday would provide *some* benefit to his mother's soul. But there was one thing still nagging at him.

"I...I...I..." His struggle with his tongue and throat continued. "I-I just d-don't get wh-what happened...It...it—"

"*Easy*..." His father turned down the radio.

"I-I just c-couldn't control my body. I—"

"You lost it, Robert, yes. It happens, in life and on life's margins. What matters is learning how to deal with it. And that's where we're heading. To school. Keep your eyes and ears open this morning. You may be blessed in getting some of the underlying lessons set in the reverend's sermon."

Robert hoped so. Even if he found almost everything else he saw and heard at this church distasteful, he always looked forward to the sermon. Rev. Richardson had come up in the traditional black Baptist preacher mold but had developed into a post-modern progressive seeking to reform a moribund, regressing church and the morbid, depressing status of the "black flock" of modern society. Robert usually hung on his every word.

His father parked in his usual spot, in the dirt lot at the trunk of the largest tree in sight. "If you feel anything...*happening* during the service," his father said as they got out of the car, "you be sure to let me know. We'll get out of there ASAP."

Robert felt something happening to him as soon as they entered the sanctuary. He grimaced and put his hand on his stomach, but said nothing. This was normal. So far, there were roughly three hundred people sitting in a room with capacity for one thousand, but Robert had no trouble spotting about a dozen folks who normally queased his stomach. Self-righteous hypocrites, vain liars, and materialistic two-facers—he complained about them often during the rides home from church, always prompting an instant rebuke and mini sermon from his father. Over the past several years, Rev. Richardson had unintentionally succeeded in driving many away with his unconventional views and rhetoric on issues of gender and sexuality. And race. And God. And Heaven and Hell. He had, in turn, attracted a small fraction of the total numbers that were lost. But a handful of those whom Robert deemed "no-gooders" weren't going anywhere, apparently.

The church organist played the welcome music that served as background noise before services were officially underway. Robert and his father nodded and half-smiled at a few people as they made their way down the aisle to a third-row pew, not too far from where many of the deacons would be sitting. His father believed the casual and friendly chitchat expected and often demanded from churchgoers should wait until after church. Robert preferred not to chitchat with anyone except Rev. Richardson and a select few deacons.

He took his seat. Before his father could do the same, three church matriarchs accosted him, two of whom were wearing ostentatious and almost comical hats. They asked how he was doing, how he was feeling, how life was treating him—the same questions the busybodies asked him every week, starting out on the surface then digging with more penetrating questions. His father politely accommodated them as Robert shook his head at the interrogation.

Many among the church regulars sincerely felt for the aggrieved and unfortunate in their midst: the widows and widowers, the unwed mothers, the recovering addicts, and so on. *But some churchgoers are just too damn nosy.* The thought flashed in Robert's head as he caught sight of two young women smiling and whispering nearby, glancing and pointing at him with their pinkies. He grabbed a book of hymns from the back of the pew in front of him and pretended to read.

"And how are you this good morning, Brother Robert?"

Damn. Time for his interrogation.

Robert looked up and saw five looking back at him—his father, the three matriarchs, and a young woman who'd joined them while he wasn't paying attention. A six-foot-tall dark chocolate beauty with shoulder-length black hair and almond-shaped eyes. His father said nothing but raised an eyebrow, signaling that he should stand up and show some respect to these ladies, to his sister-mothers in Christ.

"Good morning, Dr. Wright. Good morning, Mrs. Stevens. Good morning, Ms. Ofeni." Robert spoke and nodded at each as he rose. He then turned to greet the young woman who looked vaguely familiar, like someone he'd seen but had never actually met. She looked like she might've been a college freshman or sophomore. In what crowd could they have possibly crossed paths? "Good morning."

"*Blessed* good Sunday morning to you!" Mrs. Stevens said.

"How are you feeling, Robert?" Ms. Ofeni asked, with no trace of insincerity. "Your father said you've been sick, been in the hospital…"

"Well, yeah, briefly. I…had some kind of episode, but I'm feeling fine now, thank you."

"Thank the *Lord*," Dr. Wright said. "He's responsible! All blessings are due to *Him*!"

And curses, Robert thought, *who's responsible for them?* He swallowed and said, "Yes ma'am."

"And how did you do in your wrestling game, Robert?" Mrs. Stevens asked.

"I lost."

"Oh well." Dr. Wright sighed as she shrugged. "The Lord giveth and He taketh away. That's my *Job* speaking!"

Forget Job, Robert thought. *You should get a job minding your own damn business.*

"Such a savage barbaric sport anyway," Mrs. Stevens said.

"I never could understand why," Dr. Wright added, "if you must play a sport, you didn't do something more respectable, and likable. Like baseball. Or basketball, like your friend Herman plays."

"Whatever encouraged you," Mrs. Stevens said, "to want to participate in such a dangerous thing, such a perverse activity?"

Robert took a deep breath. They mentioned Herman but insinuated there's something wrong with *him?* "I was inspired by the story of Jacob wrestling with the angel...or was it with God?" He struggled not to smirk.

Dr. Wright and Mrs. Stevens glared at him. The young woman unknown to him seemed to smile, in an odd way. Both he and his father took notice.

"Robert," his father said as he gestured toward her, "this is Sister Artemisia." Robert smiled and nodded at her.

"One of my nieces," Dr. Wright said. "A soul in flux, I don't think she'll mind me saying." Artemisia didn't appear to mind; she seemed more interested in Robert than anything anyone else was saying. "She got into a little trouble up in Washington, so she just moved in with me—temporarily—as she gets back on track. Whatever church she was going to before, well, I'm sure her baptism didn't count for much of anything, I'll just leave it at that. While she's living with me, she's going to get rebaptized here. She needs to get her soul saved."

"Amen," Mrs. Stevens said.

"Congratulations," Robert said as he studied her, wondering why she didn't seem at all bothered by her aunt's condescension. "I'm sure you'll be very happy here."

"And everywhere *else* from now on!" Dr. Wright added. "The Lord walks next to His own at *all* times, in *all* places."

"Amen."

"I didn't expect to see you here," Artemisia said.

Robert squinted an eye and cocked his head slightly. "I'm sorry?"

"We've met before." Her brow furrowed. "Don't you remember me?" Her smile curled and crooked, replacing any note of friendliness with mischief. Robert gazed at the bizarre expression in silence.

"Wonderful!" Mrs. Stevens clapped her hands. "No need for you to feel alone now, Artemisia. You already have a friend in the church. Now you have another good excuse to keep coming."

Artemisia said nothing as she kept her gaze fixed on Robert, her lips contorting into something close to a scowl.

"And, Brother Robert," Mrs. Stevens continued, "maybe you can introduce her to your friend Herman."

"Maybe not," he distantly heard himself saying.

"Oh?" Dr. Wright asked. "And why not?"

"You want her to get saved, or enslaved?"

Robert knew what he was saying. He heard what he was saying. But *he* wasn't saying it. His subconscious had assumed control of his mouth and pushed his conscious mind, bound and gagged, to the background.

One of the matriarchs stared wide-eyed at Robert, while another shook her head and muttered something. The third, Ms. Ofeni, wore a mildly disturbed expression, as if she knew exactly what Robert was talking about but wished he'd just kept his mouth shut.

"Robert..." his father said.

"I mean...I *meant*..." He spoke as if his voice came from under a convulsing tongue. "Let's let Artemisia feel free to choose her own friends in the church," he was able to finally say. "She shouldn't feel pressured to associate with certain people..."

"Young man, *what* are you talking about?" Dr. Wright had become irate. "This is a church! The Body of God! There's no partisanship here, no sectarianism in here—and there shouldn't be!"

"Amen." Mrs. Stevens nodded, her eyes closed.

"This isn't your public high school. We're not happy with little groups amongst ourselves. The only groups we should be trying to form are Bible study groups!"

"Amen."

"And—"

"Ladies, ladies." His father held up his hands. "Please don't take my son's words out of context. He's still a little under the weather."

"He said he felt fine!" Dr. Wright protested.

"He's still sick." His father spoke more sternly. "You don't fully recover overnight from a seizure."

"Yes, Antonia," Ms. Ofeni said, "please relax. Save your ire for your colleagues downtown."

"I'm sorry, Dr. Wright," Robert said, mock-sheepishly. "I didn't mean...whatever you thought I meant."

"Yes, well, yes..." Dr. Wright was the owner of four small businesses. Success in the private sector made her very self-assured in the public and religious sectors, always willing to argue but never debate, never willing to admit error, but always willing to let everyone know where she ranked. It didn't help that she was also related to the reverend. Within church walls, her normal attitude amplified. One could tell when she had issues with others by her refusal to call them by their proper name. "I hope you feel better soon, young man," she said. "God doesn't love ugly." She turned, waved for Artemisia to follow, and walked toward a cluster of women at another pew.

His father sighed as Robert squinted at the departing duo. While Mrs. Stevens, Ms. Ofeni, and his father engaged in a whispered gossip session, he kept staring, focusing on Artemisia. He wasn't sure when, where, or whether they'd ever met, but he was sure that if they had, it wasn't a nice experience.

SILENT AT THE PULPIT, Rev. Richardson slowly turned his head from left to right, right to left, surveying the individuals who'd made an effort to attend on this dreary morning. It was customary for him to take what he called an "inventory" before beginning his sermon. He was often inspired by whom he did or didn't see, usually not in a positive way. He had to start off talking bad about someone, someone who got his blood hot. "A bad seed watered with boiling blood gives rise to a passion fruit tree," he'd once explained his method, using a phrase that impressed some with its poetry but didn't make much sense to Robert. Robert was particularly annoyed since he knew passion fruit didn't grow on trees.

"Sisters and Brothers," the reverend said, "many of you have heard about, and no doubt been disturbed by, the story of Pastor Campbell, a sick, *strange*, and scary man who was the pastor of a small church in the southern part of the state. He was arrested recently, thankfully, when it was discovered he'd been abusing his power, abusing his wife, abusing *all* the flowers in the garden he tended in God's name. He was someone who misinterpreted and neglected his marriage vows, grossly misunderstood the concept of marriage in general, and disrespected the spouses of all the married men who attended his church—chiefly his own spouse. Here was a man, a little man, a *tiny* no-good man of no god—"

"Yes, sir," said someone in the congregation.

"That's *right!*" cried another.

"—who thought all the alleged sins of Eve, were born unto, *given* unto, passed down and inherited by all the women of the world. This man would discipline, he would reprove, he would upbraid and castigate...aw, hell, he would just outright *beat* his wife! In private and in public, in the house of God and in his hole of Hell that he called his home!"

Rev. Richardson had no qualms about using "the small words" of profanity while in the pulpit. "Hell," "damn," and "bastard" were all fair game. He claimed they were biblical and entirely appropriate to whatever topic on which he was speaking when he employed them. Many didn't mind. Robert loved it. It was, however, yet another practice that pushed a few churchgoers into other houses of worship.

"This worm," the reverend continued, "who knows *nothing* of God's true word, was born unto a woman, conceived in a woman's womb, cared for and nurtured by a woman...And yet and still, and still and yet, he desired, he *designed*, he decided to blame his wife—too meek to speak out—for the alleged sins of Eve and the spiraling serpent! He wanted her to repent, he wanted *all* women to repent, he wants them to live in shame, he wants *all* women to live in shame because of a myth, an allegory, a symbolic story that some are too narrow-minded to understand. He's not too far away from the unrepentant anti-Semite who wants all Jews to be forced to 'repent' because of what a Jewish character does in the Grimm fairy tale *The Jew Among Thorns*! When we are instructed to walk in the straight-and-narrow, Brothers and Sisters, Sisters and Brothers, it does *not* mean that we should have a straight and narrow interpretation of the Good Book!"

When his father seemed to "amen" this louder than anyone else in the congregation, Robert felt compelled to start making a few vocal contributions. But when he glanced around at some of the others encouraging the reverend to "Preach!" and "Teach!" he thought it better to keep quiet than to join a chorus of some of the most morally suspect people he'd ever met.

"There is one man," the reverend said, "whose experience, whose *example*, can serve as a healthy reminder of our lot and purpose in this world. His *very life* was composed by a poetic Creator abiding by a harsh, prickly theory of poetics considered frightening and beautiful at the same time by those who know and love God and who, through that love, know that they can experience the presence of the working Word surrounding them, *within* them, penetrating and *healing* the wounds of their flesh and skin, and pushing their own spirits to transcend what we currently see as a harsh and disconnected reality. *Job—*whose very name stands for repentance...”

Job again. It seemed Dr. Wright had gotten a peek at Rev. Richardson's sermon beforehand. Robert knew the book; he hadn't read it since he'd been forced to attend Sunday school many years ago, but even then the story struck him as odd: Satan makes a deal with God and is given permission to test the faith of the righteous Job by subjecting him to all sorts of physical, mental, and social horrors, all just to prove a point—a man who praises God in light would curse him in darkness. Even through immense suffering, however, Job stays true; he doesn't curse God, but he does question his Maker.

Maybe it was something about being in this house of brick and stained glass, hearing the reverend's words so soon after the week he'd had, but Robert now had some questions for his maker. The questions descended upon him like revelatory doves. Or crows. He wanted to ask his mother just *how* he was a mistake. That he was the result of an unwanted pregnancy was clear enough. But the word “mistake” carried so much more meaning. Today, he knew in his bones he was a mistake multiplied. How could he fix himself? God miraculously cured and restored Job's possession at the end of his trials. Robert's fate, it seemed, was in his own hands.

“Before we begin in earnest, Brothers and Sisters,” the reverend said, “please, let us bow our heads in prayer. O Lord...”

Robert bowed his head, but he'd a hard time concentrating. With shut lids, his thoughts seemed to travel at the speed of light —shooting out and diving into prism-ponds, which scattered his attention even further. Every disparate thought sought out a memory with his mother; every thought searched a memory for any hint of what kind of son he was meant to be. And if he wasn't meant to be her son, then to whom did his soul belong? Could souls be created by mistake? Could they be placed by accident in the wrong body?

Rev. Richardson's booming bass of a voice provided background noise to Robert's mental travels. But it was another sound, a sort of muffled laughing coming from nearly the same direction as the prayer, that pulled Robert's attention back to his physical surroundings.

He opened an eye and raised his head. He shouldn't have been surprised. The source was in the choir stand behind the altar. Herman. Church was one of the few places he shed his do-rag and let his cornrows show. Now, with closed eyes and bowed head, he wore a childish grin as his right hand reached over to grab the breast of a girl sitting next to him before quickly returning to clasp the left hand resting in his lap. The muffled laughing came from the girl on Herman's left who'd been grabbed, then from the girl on the right when she was similarly fondled. Herman just grinned silently as he alternated between the girls without breaking his rhythm, without once missing his targets in spite of his shut eyes.

Robert opened his other eye and looked around. There wasn't a single individual who seemed aware of, let alone disturbed by, Herman's antics. He may've been the only one to see what was going on, but was he also the only one to hear it? Rev. Richardson didn't seem bothered by the sounds coming from behind him. He kept on with his prayer without any hint of annoyance. None of the deacons, the ushers, the nurses, or the ultrasensitive matriarchs of the church seemed to pick up on what was happening either. Surely, the latter would be the most perturbed at the slightest sign of disrespect during any portion of the service, not the least during one of the "open communications with God;" they'd go so far as to run up to the offender the second the prayer was over, snatch him by the ear, and drag him outside the church for a good stern talking-to. Robert had seen it before, but never with Herman. The goof had often played around during church services, but he'd never once been publicly humiliated. When individuals in the congregation were doing something they had no business doing while the reverend was preaching, the reverend had a habit of calling out the miscreants by weaving their names into the sermon, painting them as examples of those wildly astray from the right paths and in need of strong and serious correction. Robert knew it was just gossamer to hope that today would be Herman's time to be humiliated.

"Amen," Rev. Richardson said.

"Amen," people in the congregation responded in near unison.

Most eyes went to the reverend as he began to preach, but Robert focused on Herman. He didn't understand why hardly anyone else saw what he was seeing. Herman was now molesting any female within reach, snatching at hair, shoulders, arms, breasts, and thighs. The girls jumped a little each time Herman's hands got a good-but-brief hold on them. The older members of the choir still somehow remained oblivious to all of this while those closer to Herman's age looked on, grinning at the spectacle.

He couldn't understand, but Robert had had enough of it. He looked away from the choir and away from the reverend, searching for a sign that someone was set to make a mad dash up there and smack some sense into Herman. It was hopeless. No one in the congregation seemed to give a damn. But one girl did seem to take an interest in Robert.

Artemisia. Her mouth's corners curved upward when Robert's eyes met hers. A chill ran across his nerves as her smile distorted in such a way that Robert couldn't help but think, *Cheshire tigress.*

He didn't turn away. He didn't even consider it as he watched the strange face and listened to Rev. Richardson's reading from the Book of Job. The words came in clear and resounding, as if the reverend were sitting next to him, talking in a slow, measured manner. The verses were all he heard; Artemisia's face was all he saw.

Robert's temples, temporal lobe, and other parts inside and out throbbed as verses mixed with new sounds. Clinking bottles. They were inside his head. Intuitively, he perceived twelve of them, multicolored, some half empty, others a quarter empty, a few a third empty. The clinking increased until it was all he could hear. He grimaced but didn't turn away from Artemisia's contorted face staring back at him.

He knew he was losing it, descending into another episode. He had to alert his dad. He had to get out of the church before another epileptic fit seized him and took down everyone near him. His legs twitched to stand, but the twitching in his nose was stronger, forcing him to sneeze, shattering all of the battling bottles in his head. Stained-glass shards and multivalent water flooded his consciousness before evaporating in a blink.

And in a blink, everything changed. He'd an odd feeling that several minutes had passed instead of a mere second. Checking his watch proved nothing; the battery had been dead for two days. But things had certainly changed.

Artemisia was looking at the Bible in her lap, her face expressionless. She almost appeared to be napping. Even if not, it seemed she'd been settled in this position for some time. She was one of the very few not looking at the reverend as he wound up his sermon in his usual hyper style, spreading an infectious mood caught by most in the congregation. Even Herman was now a rapt listener, his eyes not deviating from the reverend for even a moment. Artemisia's gaze remained on the book in her lap, her body not shifting an inch.

Was he imagining this, or had he imagined what had happened before he sneezed? His mind and body were still under attack, but it seemed the nature of the attacks had shifted. As if to underscore this revelation, Robert sneezed again and opened his eyes to a mass of crimson dots, spots of spittle that flashed, fell, and faded to nothing. The next sound he heard was Rev. Richardson asking everyone to bow their heads for the final prayer. The sermon was over. His sneeze must have pushed time-flow forward. How? *In this house of brick and stained glass...*

He pondered with his eyes open, seeing nothing but blurs as the concluding prayer sounded like a continuous rumbling in his ears. It was all a distant thunder, only calmed when the choir stood to sing "God Put a Rainbow in the Sky."

2

Robert had stumbled out of the church, positive his father and others were speaking to him, but in too low a mood to pay any heed. He just wanted to go home. He'd walked in an indirect line, reminiscent of his pattern in Brian's backyard a week ago. But this time it wasn't checkers; he was playing chess against himself. He didn't stop until he was about twenty feet from the car, parked under that massive tree. That big winter tree, awaiting spring. A giant undead plant.

It was leafless, so he'd no idea what kind of tree it was. But standing there, something preventing him from moving another step, he let his thoughts play and imagined blood mangoes—or some stranger fruits—hanging from the tree, ready to bomb the car below. He knew there really was no fruit on the tree, and none would magically appear. But something within him, and something without—probably the boisterous throng of hypocrites in front of the church several dozen feet behind him—compelled him to stare and imagine something not quite of this world.

Back during his junior high years—when he was sick, in bed, and on cold medicine—he developed the ability to manipulate his dreams. He'd alter the scenery, shift time, teleport himself from one place to another, split himself up in order to exist in several different forms so he could do several different things in several different locations all at once. He wasn't pumped up with medicine now, and he wasn't asleep. He wasn't sure where he was mentally. But, on a whim, he tried to see just how much control he could exercise over a mere daydream.

He imagined the tree's fruit becoming paler, stranger than mangoes or anything native to America. The color drained as the plump shape gave way to a longer, thinner form, appearing finally as crystal-clear drill bits.

Robert had conjured this vision, but shortly after having arrived, it went its own way. He gazed at the massive, crooked tree as indigo lightning streaked from sky to ground, splitting the skeletal tree into halves.

The right half of the tree flushed with red, yellow, and orange icicles, each one a long thin ice drill of *fiery* colors, throbbing with a brightness that pulsated and glistened.

The left half of the tree had icicle drill bits that neither flushed nor burned; they just turned at an imperceptible speed, ready to drill into something. Or someone.

As if on cue, a patch of ground between the two tree halves trembled and cracked open. Time crept as something climbed out, freeing itself from the body and soil of the earth. It stood erect after slowly emerging, though the soles of its feet were still connected to roots under the ground's surface.

This genderless humanoid, senses and skin still tender from its birth, felt about, reaching its arms to its sides, touching both trees with the tips of its fingers before bringing both hands to its chest. The left hand dug into its skin and peeled it away, making a hole big enough for the right hand to go inside, pull out, and hold up...a piece of fruit.

The fruit's skin and flesh were transparent; Robert saw right through to the seeds at the core. The hand holding it extended toward Robert. In response to the offer, he only blinked.

A breeze picked up and whistled. The limbs and branches of both trees writhed and twisted, snatching and entangling the humanoid. The crystalline fruit fell as tree limbs jerked their captive up and away from the ground, snapping its feet off from their roots.

The trees' rotating icicles drilled into the humanoid's skin. Elastic tree limbs coiled around and tied themselves to the humanoid's extremities. Cold wood invaded the drill holes as other fingerless limbs whipped across the humanoid's back, stomach, and legs, trying to whip it into total submission. The humanoid struggled, but it lost more and more of its mobility as its ripe body bled diluted nectar.

Whatever was once pure about the humanoid was pure no more. Whirling icicles drilled farther and farther into the being, making its entire body glow as the autumnal lights combined into one swirling color. The body inflated like a balloon as the skin hardened into stained glass. Through the imperfect window, Robert detected flickering hints of fire. Whatever liquid was inside the humanoid rapidly converted, steaming through the cracks on the body.

The trees' branches and limbs suddenly snapped, dropping the stained and brittle corpse, as the remaining limbs and branches snatched at one another, merging again into one big, half-dead tree.

Robert closed his eyes and breathed deeply, wondering where the vision and its possible meaning had come from. Sure, he willed the beginning of the hallucination, but it had quickly taken on a life of its own, so to speak. Now that it was over, he recalled the *Paradise Lust* art project, wondering about an appropriate title for what he'd just created in his head: the Tree of Sexual Knowledge versus the Tree of a Lying Life, with an innocent being caught in the middle of it all, screwed against his—or her—will. Maybe a title like, *In Eden's Bed, A Bad Seed...*

"Remembering me?"

He almost jumped when he heard the whisper in his right ear. His eyes jerked open, but he knew the voice before he even saw her. Artemisia had managed to sidle up to him. He was so entwined in his own thoughts, he didn't notice her standing just a few inches away.

Her smile shifted into different angles of crookedness as her almond eyes seemed to flash. He hadn't noticed before, but her irises were burnt orange.

"How—? Do we—?" His trouble with words continued. "Did we really meet? I mean, before today?"

She cocked her head, as if thinking he had to be joking. "Multiple times. In multiple places. Multiple ways."

All of those ways and places and times had to involve parties, maybe even some of Brian's. But why couldn't he remember? He'd never taken drugs or drank alcohol, so he couldn't have been high or drunk when they'd met. Still, some of the high capacity parties he'd attended could be overwhelming, particularly the summertime block parties. It was possible they'd been introduced, even exchanged a few words, but taken in with all of his other experiences, he could've easily forgotten her.

He never would've forgotten those burnt-orange eyes, though. Were they contacts? Had she put them in after the church service?

"I'm sorry I don't—"

"Each time we've met," Artemisia said, "I've done everything I thought necessary, but it still hasn't been enough, hasn't made much of a difference. But I've had time to study. I didn't expect to see you this morning. I'm not ready to dance with you yet. But soon. And this time will be the last time."

He may've never have taken drugs, but he figured she had to be on something.

She turned to leave. He should've let her, but he couldn't stop himself.

"What exactly are you talking about?" he asked.

She turned again, looking him in the eyes.

"Ending the enemy of the once-and-future world, Junior Adam. Your names change, but your soul doesn't." Her eyes definitely flashed this time, as if a match had been struck just behind her pupils. Pumpkin eyes.

Robert's head swam. *Junior Adam?* This nut had him confused with someone else.

"Hey, Goldner!"

Another familiar voice called from several feet away. *Shit.* One nut fast approaching, while the other couldn't leave soon enough.

"What's up, my man?" Herman grinned as he extended his hand to shake.

Robert wanted to slam his fist into his jaw. "Get the hell out of here."

"Whoa!" Herman held up his hands as if Robert had pulled a knife on him. "Watch those words, Brother—we're on the Lord's property! We *are* the Lord's property! Weren't you listening to Reverend Chicken Gizzard in there?" He then turned to Artemisia and looked her up and down, settling his gaze on her waist. "So, ain't you going to introduce me?"

"No," Robert said. "Go away."

Artemisia didn't glance once in Herman's direction, as if he didn't even exist. "You judge," she said to Robert, "dwelling on the immorality and hypocrisies of others, most of it just imagined, conjured up in your diseased mind. All of it to avoid looking deeper within. Your self-hatred is warranted. You'll be out of your misery soon." Her orange eyes flashed once more as she said, "I'll be seeing you," and turned to walk toward the church.

"See me, baby!" Herman called after her. "Come see *me* with your badass self!"

Robert gazed after her, half expecting she'd melt away, like a fading dream.

"Who was *that*?" Herman asked.

"Someone from Planet Nut," Robert mumbled.

"Yeah? Well, I'd like to rock her world with *my* nuts!"

"Your stupid ass deserves her."

"I sure do!"

Robert looked at him. *Really* looked at him. The two of them went way back. He'd seen him in so many different lights before. But now his thoughts went insanely wild, like they had earlier when focusing on memories with his mother. This time, however, his thoughts raced and touched upon every antiblack slur he'd ever heard, and a few he even made up on the spot. He couldn't stop or control his thoughts, only try to keep them from infecting his words.

"What the hell do you want, Herman?"

"Hey, I just came to see if you're okay. I heard you were sick or somethin'. And, man, you must be if you let a hot chick like *that* go and get away from you!"

"I didn't *let* her get away. I *wanted* her to go away. Just like I want you to."

"Calm down, man, geez!" He again held up his hands as if he were being mugged. "Seriously, man, are you all right? You're still lookin' a li'l rough."

"I'm fine."

"Are you sure? I heard about what happened."

Robert let his guard down. "What did you hear?"

"Last week at the tournament. They're sayin' you got down and freaked out."

"Who's 'they'?"

"Everyone. At Brian's party on Friday, some dudes were sayin' that you picked up a guy, carried him over to the bleachers and then threw him into the crowd. I was like, 'Oh, shit! That fool Goldner may actually have a li'l coolness left in him!'"

Robert shook his head. Was he making this up?

"Then they said you jumped up on the announcers' table, started beatin' your chest and pickin' up chairs and throwin' 'em around. I was like, 'All right! My *man!* Takin' it to 'em!'"

"*What?*"

"And then, when security came, they said you started break dancin' and I said—"

"Okay, just shut the hell up. None of that's true and you know it."

"Well, I know you can't dance worth shit, and you aren't strong enough to throw anyone far into anywhere, but people are talkin'..."

"People are idiots. You, that crazy-ass girl who was just here, whoever you were talking to at that dumb-ass party, all those assholes over there—" Robert waved in the general direction of the church, then stopped. His mood was taking him too far, too deep into a hateful place he really didn't want to go. He was being pushed. He had to push back.

"Oh, *I'm* an idiot?" Herman asked. "I tell you I'm concerned about your well-being, I let you know some people are up to no good and are smokin' up stories and rumors about you, and you call me an 'idiot' for all this?"

Robert shook his head. "I'm sorry. I just don't feel well."

"You just said you were fine."

An echo. As soon as Herman said it, Robert remembered someone else had said it earlier, in the same tone. *Dr. Wright,* aunt of Artemisia and relative of Rev. Richardson...who was also Robert's relative. Could that crazy girl be related to him in some way? A cousin? The cousin that had slaughtered his mother had fled from the scene and never been found. Robert didn't remember her name—but, hell, six years ago, Artemisia would've been too young to match the description. Or would she? What *was* the description?

His head hurt. His brain pulsed. The organ in his skull expanded and contracted like a heart at rest. Herman was long gone from his vision, as was the church; in their place, a dense forest of redwoods cropped up, the space between each tree no wider than a needle's eye. He knew they weren't real, but looking closer, he saw the trees formed a ring; a pond lay hidden at the center. He knew that if he could only reach it and dive in, he might find some truth about Artemisia, her realities and her lies. Was he in any way connected to her? Was she in any way connected with the greatest tragedy of his life? Had she mistaken his identity? *Junior Adam?*

"—gorilla in a garden!"

Herman's exclamation jerked Robert to the here-and-now. "What? What did you say?"

"You," Herman said. "If you'd actually made it to State, you've would've embarrassed the rest of us acting like a gorilla in a garden."

Robert's eyes narrowed. His heart rate doubled. He took a step forward. "Who the *fuck* are you to be talking about somebody else being an embarrassment?"

Herman looked him up and down, then sneered. "That's your problem, Goldnerd. Always been your problem. Thinkin' you're so much better than everyone else. Especially blacks. Doin' everything you can to make yourself different from the rest of us, as if difference, *any* kind of difference, is better than being a part of us."

"Herman, I swear—"

"That chick that was just here was right. You hate yourself so much you don't even see yourself. Or anyone else. You don't accept reality, so you make the shit up. Just look at you. The way you talk. The way you act. That bullshit music that you listen to. The way you think—"

"And that's your problem." Robert jabbed his finger at Herman's face. "Everything *you* say and think is bullshit and nonsense. Reality to you is a white supremacist's dream."

A broad smile replaced Herman's sneer. "And what do you dream about? That super-pale scarecrow Leigh? You prefer her over that black-and-beautiful chick who was just here?" He took a step closer. "What reality are you really trying to make up?"

Robert stood his ground. If Herman wanted to throw, he wouldn't back away.

"What do you think her parents would do if they knew about you?" Herman asked. "What would your father do?"

"I don't give a shit." It seemed all the blood in Robert's head was draining into his hands. He balled them into fists. *Deliver me from evil.*

Herman eyed the fists and grinned. "I've noticed. Your shitty little secret isn't much of a secret. Half the school knows, but parents are just willin' themselves blind."

Robert so wanted to punch him blind right now.

"But I know you," Herman said, grinning again. "You're a smart darky. Smarter than the rest of us. Or so you think. But I figured it out a while ago. I think a lot of people have. It's just a ruse. A thin white secret about a thin white girl, meant to cover up your real secret. Robert and Leigh—who gives a shit? But Robert and Davin, and who knows how many others—"

Robert cocked his right hand, but it was as if some invisible hook prevented him from following through, smashing his fist into Herman's eye. He'd no qualms about fighting on church grounds, but he didn't want his father and Herman's mother as his audience. The two were fast approaching the boys; they had a clear line of sight but were apparently oblivious to what had been happening. Herman was right about one thing: some parents willed themselves blind.

"Herman," Robert's father said with a wide smile and extended hand, "how are you doing today?"

"Fine, Mr. Goldner, just fine." Herman returned the smile as he shook. "And how are you?"

"Doing well, doing well. Nice performance up there in the choir today, as usual."

"Thank you, sir," Herman said. "I always try my best to represent myself and my Lord properly."

Robert glared.

"And hello, young man." Herman's mother spoke with an irritated tone. Understandable. Robert had completely forgotten his manners.

"Hello, Mrs. Harrison," he said. "How are you?"

"Just fine." She returned his smile. "How are *you* this morning?"

"A little exhausted," he said. "My head is still pounding."

"Oh, that's too bad. Your father was telling me that you've been sick."

"Yes, ma'am." He glanced at Herman. "I feel plagued."

"Well, let's get you home and put you to bed," his father said. He turned to give Herman's mother a hug.

Herman put his hand on Robert's shoulder and leaned in close to whisper. "Try not to let any dudes in with you."

Robert shrugged his hand off as Herman snickered and walked away. *Deliver me from...*

"Be well, Robert." Herman's mother hugged him. "There are too few good men living in this world. We can't have you crossing over to the other side prematurely."

"No, ma'am." Robert hugged her with his eyes closed. When he opened them, they focused on the tree next to his father's car. For a moment, it seemed some of the limbs were waving at him.

3

"Robert, please," his father said, "just finish eating."

"I *can't*." He also couldn't refuse pounding his fist on the table.

Robert had moaned, tossed, and turned for ten hours in bed on Sunday night. As he trudged to the breakfast table Monday morning, his father made it clear he was worried about his health and suggested Robert skip school. Robert was more worried about the surprise physics test due to occur any day now. They eventually compromised, agreeing Robert would go to school but skip wrestling practice—though Robert fully intended to forget his side of the promise. Breakfast had continued peacefully for sixty seconds, the amount of time it took for his father to finish his toast then compliment Herman's singing in church.

"What's the matter with you?" his father asked. "Where's all this coming from?"

"Him! *Them!* Negative stereotypes...They make us look bad in the eyes of *everyone*. And Herman profits from it!"

His father crooked an eyebrow. "Profits from it?"

"He's praised by the people who should know better. Almost

everyone likes him, loves him even. Classmates, teachers, all the girls, grown women—"

"Ah, there it is," his father leaned back in his chair and smiled. "Jealousy. The same theme from various stories of lives and loves."

"It's not jealousy." He wanted to pound that fist again, but experience told him his father would only allow him to get away with one. "He gets a pass on everything he does because he's so entertaining."

"Robert, you and Herman have been friends for over a decade—"

"We're *not* friends."

"And his mother and I have been friends for more than twice as long. I don't know if your memory is going or what, but you two were very close when you were children. Best friends. Did everything together, went everywhere together. Your friendship brought our families closer together. And still, even back then, inseparable as you were, you two teased each other. That's how boys bond. Heck, that's even how men bond. You should hear me and some of my buddies going at it at work." His father chuckled before raising his cup to his lips.

Robert picked up a chunk of banana from his bowl with his spoon. "I'd like to go at Herman with a machete."

His father swallowed his coffee and got serious.

"Robert, that's not funny. You need to watch it. Black males in this society are an endangered species. Far too many are locked up or are being murdered or die mysteriously. *Far* too many, way ahead of their time."

"And *far* too many who are free-and-living put an emphasis on jive-timing and trying to be *supa* cool while harassing those of us who're interested in the life of the mind...creativity and intelligence. Anyone can *be* as bad as he or she wants, but I don't like anyone making us *look* bad. Why do we have to tolerate it? You always used to say the image is extremely important when you're part of a minority group. One, two, or just a few will be seen as reps of all. Their kind is taking all of us back—"

"*Their* kind?" His father gave him a look he'd only seen him deliver once before: to a racist Spanish teacher his freshman year. "Now, Robert, don't lose yourself and go down the road of self-hatred. Remember *Invisible Man*—"

"I'm not on any path to *self*-hatred. It's them. Why are you defending them? They're a minority group within a minority, a self-destructive bunch that's poisoning the rest of the group. And Herman's a perfect example of what's wrong—he's the ultimate Mr. Wrong!" He didn't like to argue with his father. More often they engaged in a healthy debate over music, where they ended up agreeing to disagree but not before learning something from each other. But this was no debate. Robert was right and it was important to make his father see that. If his father, the man who had raised him to be intelligent and responsible, didn't agree with him on this, then the father-son relationship was damaged.

"Please eat something now." It seemed his father was tired of listening. Robert, however, was just catching his second wind.

"He represents everything you've always lectured against becoming. Why're you excusing this guy?"

His father took a slow sip of coffee. "I hear what you're saying, and you're partly right. But it's tough for us in this environment today."

"And people like Herman are just making it tougher."

"He's surviving."

"By destroying the best of us."

"Sounds like someone's got a superiority complex."

"Yeah, these proud-to-be-ignorant blacks who spend all their time screwing around—"

"That's *enough*, Robert. You need to get off that high horse of yours. You're no saint, either. I may keep quiet, turn the other eye and all that, but I'm well aware of some of the fooling around that you do. And I'm telling you now, stop being so obsessed with

Herman. It's unnatural." His father lowered his eyes as his voice drowned in his coffee cup.

Robert also shut up, swallowing back the rest of his bile and bitterness. His father had warned him about self-hatred and obsession; Herman had already accused him of both. Herman was easy to dismiss, but his father...Was he right? Were *they* right?

He picked up his spoon and looked down at his bowl. Despite having no appetite, he forced himself to eat the rest of the fruit, if only to keep his mouth busy.

HE'D SPENT at least thirty minutes by his locker before school, waiting for Leigh and watching the crowds. At times, he wondered whether he was in the right place. Had the school changed, or was he now just paying a different sort of attention?

The halls were the same, but some of the cliques walking them seemed altered. Goths, when they sneered, seemed to have fangs. Not the fake plastic ones they stuck in every Friday the thirteenth to spook the stupid, but real ones—though he convinced himself it was just a superior type of plastic. The cheerleaders, no longer content to brag of their status with short skirts, tight shirts, and flamboyant hairstyles, now actually carried a pom-pom in one hand and their books in the other, as if books were weapons, their pom-poms shields, and the classroom was a battleground. The Jewish baldies still looked the same, though now there were six of them; rather than red, white, and black, the sixth one wore a rainbow-patterned yarmulke, yet another kind of target. The slumber party had seemingly tripled in size, or maybe just an unusual number of kids had woken up late this morning. And the evangelicals, who'd always carried a Bible atop their textbooks, now carried a different black book. When a group of them had passed Robert earlier, he glanced at the cover: *Untitled*, by Brother Goldner. He knew he couldn't have seen that correctly. On second thought, after they had long passed, he was sure the book's cover had read: *On Tithing*, by Brother Goldmire.

Still, he felt that something had changed. There'd been a slight shift in reality. Well, why not? Fads changed in the blink of an eye; it made sense that high school cliques would change their numbers and personal styles just as quickly. Yet on this particular morning, the shift was unsettling, all the more so because the security guards seemed to be wearing different uniforms, more official-looking, with bronze badges over their heart. One thing he hadn't seen in all this time was Leigh, that unique clique of one with her ever-present bow. By the time the warning bell rang, he almost had a hunger to see her. Would it be the usual, or something off the charts? Apparently, he'd have to wait to find out.

He walked to class, wondering where she could be. Was she sick? What if he'd given her whatever he had? *Impossible.* While listening to music on his laptop last night, he'd convinced himself that, whatever was wrong with him, the root cause was psychological anxiety. With the unknown status of Davin, an important wrestling tournament, and academic and social pressures all weighing on him, it was all just too much. And the breakouts on his skin, the spasms, and the headaches weren't dissimilar from what he'd experienced leading up to his nervous attack several years ago in junior high. Whatever he had, it wasn't contagious. And after his climatic crackup-breakdown last week, he was definitely on the recovery end. A few more days of headaches and dizziness, fatigue and restless sleep, a weird hallucination or two, and he'd be completely back to normal.

His relationship with Leigh wouldn't be. It was over. He just wanted to apologize and end it on a positive note. That would take courage he wasn't sure he had yet.

"THERE'S a lot to be afraid of out there, people. A *lot* to get and keep you scared."

Mr. Myers stood in front of his desk with both hands on his hips. He looked bemused as he stared over the students' heads, as if he were straining to read something posted on the back wall. He'd been doing this for almost ten minutes as others, curious, turned every so often to find the wall bare and whisper jokes about senility.

"All these undercover diseases...It's serious now. You can get infected not even knowin' how, not even knowin' you got anything, right?"

Yeah, Robert thought, *this is the right way to end the course on sexual education. Strike fear into the adolescent hearts, as if those who were in the mood for experimentation—or, in some cases, reexperimentation—would be scared off by Myers's dire warnings. Funny. Just like the idea to begin the sex education course on Valentine's Day.*

It all should've ended last week, but with Mr. Myers absent on Thursday and Friday, a substitute teacher subjected the class to two standard and woefully outdated videos, the contents of which, Robert guessed, didn't approach anywhere near the subject matter of the slide show the class was set to view today. They'd been forewarned. Not only were students required to get a permission slip signed by one parent or legal guardian and two witnesses in order to be able to participate in the course, but they also had to get another signed permission slip to even be allowed inside the classroom for today's presentation.

"*Millions* of people, each year, contract a venereal disease. Some potentially fatal, some not. Some treatable, some incurable. But *all* serious."

Robert stopped scribbling zigzag and squiggle patterns on his notebook as he detected a slight change in Mr. Myers's tone.

"And people your age, you're just enterin' the beginnin' of the range of people who are most at risk, right? No one expects perfection, but we do expect you to exercise some self-control. Because this is *serious*, people. One screwup that seems like a minor screwup and you could end up screwed for *life*."

This warning elicited snickers and chortles from many in the room, but not Robert. He heard something in that tone of voice. He lifted his head from his notebook and saw a frowning Mr. Myers staring back at him, the corrugated lines on his forehead resembling some of Robert's doodles.

"I...*it* doesn't care about your race, your class, your so-called orientations or whatever. Venereal diseases only care if you're careless, if you're sloppy, if you're *stupid*, and you don't think. You lose control and let your body go any which way because the excitement is too much, you can't handle it...you get lucky, get farther than you expected, get ahead of yourself and think about glory, right?"

What the hell—? Robert thought. *He's lost it. No. I lost it. And as a result, we lost it.* Apparently, after his episode last Thursday, the tournament went straight downhill for the Howard Phillips Warriors. That's what all the bullshit was about. Coach wasn't waiting until practice. He was going to spend a good chunk of class time bitching about Robert, but not at him. And at practice, he'd journey through a three-hour hell he'd never before experienced.

"I can't control you," Mr. Myers said. "Your parents can't. The police, the government can't. You have to take responsibility for your own persons, your own bodies, your own personal private lives and activities."

Stone-faced, Robert gazed at his teacher-coach as the latter gazed back, stopped talking, and took a moment to swallow. Mr. Myers then looked toward the back of the room again, focusing this time on the slide projector. He walked toward it as he continued speaking.

"You, your generation, you people have more than a 50

percent chance of acquiring at least one venereal disease in your lifetime. Might be serious; might not be. Might lead to cancer; might cause something to fall off. Probably won't be curable. But may be treatable...at least *may* be if modern medicine is aware of it, right?

"These slides are brand new. Just received them last summer. They're pretty graphic but, I believe, necessary. And the school board believes it, too. So if you have a problem, don't run home cryin' to your parents about *me*, okay?"

Mr. Myers's voice trailed off into mumbling as he fumbled with the slide projector, a years-old model the school had purchased just last month. The material the class had to see was allegedly not available on DVD. Robert knew for a fact similar material was available in that format, but modern educational films probably weren't graphic enough for the ends the twisted school board had in mind.

He wasn't necessarily looking forward to seeing the slides, but he was anticipating the darkness. The dim lights would help his thoughts trail off and away from this pointless presentation. He didn't need to take notes or pay much attention; there'd be no class test on sex or its consequences—*that* the school administrators wouldn't allow. As only about 60 percent of those eligible any given semester took the sexual education course, testing was deemed unfair.

After a few more minutes of grumbling, Mr. Myers finally got the projector ready. "Now instead of screwin' around, maybe your generation can start here, before it's too late to see. Go and stay straight, focusin' on what *really* matters. Goldner, get the lights."

Robert hobbled to the light switch, flicked it, and walked with a less noticeable limp back to his seat. His left foot had apparently fallen asleep. He hoped he wouldn't do the same, or at least not snore if he did. He didn't want to embarrass himself in front of Coach again.

Mr. Myers projected the first image onto the screen, big and bright. "This is scabies."

Robert stared at the magnified patch of skin behind someone's knees, with its numerous red bumps and lines, as he listened to the common ways one could contract the disease. Mr. Myers lingered on this first slide for a full minute before clicking to slides featuring the bumpy rash under someone's armpits, at someone's waistline, between someone's fingers, and finally on some guy's genitals. Most students groaned.

"That's *right*," Mr. Myers said. "That's what you can get if you act *stupid*. Now here's syphilis."

He clicked to slides showing a close-up of a rash on a man's arm, then a rash on a woman's leg, then on the palms of someone's hands, before finally getting to a slide showing several wart-like lesions in a man's genital area. Robert felt a twinge in his stomach. He winced as others in the classroom groaned. This last image remained on the screen while Mr. Myers explained the several stages of syphilis in detail. Robert's abdominal muscles undulated, producing a series of tiny pinches on his stomach. His breathing became irregular as his heartbeat skipped and sped up at random.

When Mr. Myers moved on to gonorrhea, Robert's heartbeat and breathing resumed their near-normal pace, despite the fact he was looking at skin lesions on someone's leg, small pus-filled sores planted on a patch of red, irritated skin. He viewed the images through blurry vision as he struggled to ignore Mr. Myers's words, but they still had an effect. He felt queasy. When the projector switched to a slide of genital-area blisters resulting from herpes, he closed his eyes, switching his blurred vision of the slides to *no* vision. But the rumbling and churning in his stomach didn't stop; the area felt warm. Robert groaned, blaming it all on yesterday's carelessness.

He'd wondered about it on Sunday evening but didn't care too much. Now he realized it wasn't such a great idea to quit his seasonal vegetarian diet so soon, only a few days after his wrestling season had ended. It would have been easy, incredibly easy, to eat the spaghetti his father had prepared without the gourmet meatballs. But his daze hadn't quite dissipated. Sunday dinner served as his only break from studying physics. A conjunction of physical weakness and absentmindedness caused him to succumb and indulge in a minor feast of first meats. He was in a dizzying zone all throughout the meal.

And now he felt it, the upset grumbling of a steadily approaching storm. Below, down deep in the stomach, from where Sunday's supper should have long ago departed, something writhed and twisted. He closed his eyes, tightly, until he imagined a ball of wriggling strings emerging from his small intestine, struggling its way back into his stomach.

Robert squinted harder, pushing the blood out of his eyelids as his inner vision sharpened, getting closer to see exactly what it was that had jumped off course, able to resist digestion and disrespect such a powerful flow through the tract. Distantly, he heard a voice whispering in his head—*"What you see is reality"*—as tears trickled down his cheeks and he got a good view of the problem: a tangle of tiny worms, back-crawling their way to the pit of his stomach.

His face contorted as he focused, making out two distinct strands comprising the malformed sphere. Red worms and black worms—or, more poetically, heartworms and earthworms. A glistening slime, possibly resulting from continual secretion, enabled the worms to stick together and move against their environment's will as they continued their invasion into the stomach, finally settling in the pit.

The worms writhed and wriggled furiously, each one elongating as they twisted around one another, black earthworms intertwining with red heartworms, threading, embracing each other so tightly they interpenetrated each other. Earths in hearts, hearts in earths—earths, hearts, earths, hearts—they were *repro-*

ducing, giving instantaneous birth to tinier red and black worms that plumped and elongated, wriggled and writhed, struggled with and strangled one another, becoming hopelessly entangled with one another.

Robert squeezed the sides of his desk as he shook his head. The tussling in his stomach's pit only became more vivid in his mind. The spectacle of worms copulating, rolling and roiling in his stomach's rotten jelly, forced him to open his eyes, only to be confronted with the image of cauliflowerlike genital warts sprouting around someone's ass.

The thunder-thumping of his heart increased as his bowels violently shifted and growled. Overpopulated, the stomach forced some of the sticky worms to the nearest underpopulated region. Robert sprang up from his seat, tripped, and almost fell when his foot glanced against his desk leg. He caught his balance and sprinted for the door as the heads of the first three worms oozed up and reached the back of his tongue.

Dashing into the hall, he heard a chorus of strange, deep laughter coming from behind. It followed him all the way to the restroom's door.

ROBERT COULDN'T MAKE it to the stall. He was lucky enough to get to the nearest sink as remnants of breakfast then dinner made their push up the esophagus, over the tongue, and past his lips. Whatever clique had been chilling in the restroom when he burst in fled at the first sight, if not the sounds, of regurgitation. Robert's hands squeezed the sink's cold and hot water knobs, keeping a firm grasp even after he'd rotated both to their limits. The water pressure was unusually low—a small blessing as, with minor exceptions, it prevented the water and its ingredients from splashing back onto him.

They weren't worms. Just food. His imagination was a bitch.

The smell, however, was very real, and the water did nothing to mask it. Even though his eyelids shut so tight that tears had trouble escaping, the odor that wafted into his nostrils evoked images of carrion. And it wasn't going away; his disgorge had clogged the drain. Before the next heave, he moved to a sink farther down along the range.

Minutes passed. A few times, he heard the bathroom door swing open and six or seven footsteps, followed by *"Damn!"* or *"Shit!"* By the time the fourth person entered, shouted, and exited, Robert hunched over a third sink, alternating between coughing and trying to spit out the tiny chunks lodged in his mouth's nooks and crannies. He barely had strength to stand, let alone keep balance. But he felt steady enough to wipe tears from the corners of his eyes and splash warm water into his mouth. He then looked in the mirror for the first time.

His skin was not its usual oak-tree brown. It looked more like tree bark suffering from white fungal rot—brown overlaid with a thin white film.

He gaped. He could only take short breaths through his mouth. A tight buzzing at the back of his skull quickened and was answered by a pounding at his temples. Robert clenched his teeth, forced himself to take deeper breaths and keep his balance.

Something sharp jabbed the base of his skull and at the middle of his forehead, as if two tiny shards had broken off from his skull and into his skin. He winced and held his breath. In the mirror, his skin dried and tightened. The buzzing at the back of his skull subdued as the pounding at his temples fell into a rhythm, increasing in intensity.

His nostrils flared. His eyes bulged as his skin drew tighter to the bone. His lips drew back to reveal full rows of teeth as his gums faded from pink to white to translucent before receding altogether into the roots.

The insistent driving rhythm of "Time—Untie Me" coursed through his brain as his face's skin grew ashen and turned to patches of gray and black. Tiny colored blood vessels were now visible, pulsing circuits that glowed indigo and orange, yellow and blue.

Robert didn't think to scream. He didn't think much of anything. There was no room. The dirgelike music and turgid lyrics of "Time—Untie Me" took up every available space in his head. He could only gaze. His eyes appeared as frosted black-and-white stones as his vision blurred, faded, only to become crystal clear again once his skin was completely ash.

Flakes of it, a few at a time, detached from his face and floated to the sink. The pounding, *screeching*, booming music in his head shook off more and more. He watched, thoughtless, speechless, as salt-and-pepper hair from his scalp, his eyebrows, and his eyelashes detached and joined the flurry.

His blood and fluids and pus that had hardened to crust also began to flake, joining the hairs and ashen flesh sprinkling the faucet and sink. But as the fallout continued, becoming denser, the nature of the journey changed. The detritus paused in midair then sparked, flared into fuchsia and disappeared, never reaching the sink.

He couldn't blink. His lids, lips, and nose were gone. The ears were going fast. And his eyes...He looked dead on at them in the mirror. They weren't stones. They were near-clear spheres of ice encasing a tiny black...*something*. Whatever they were, they weren't frozen. The black specks stuttered and stopped, stuttered and stopped, gaining in speed until vibrating nonstop, contributing to his difficulty in determining what they were.

He hadn't the presence of mind to process it anyway. The knowledge would be no more or less relevant than the fact that his flesh—every layer of skin and muscle and other tenuous attachments—was all but gone. All that remained was a skull of onyx with random spots and streaks of glittering crimson, dried remnants of some kind of blood. He couldn't move his eyes to see below the bottom tip of his lower jaw. He was unaware of what, if anything, had happened to the rest of his body.

But the skull—*his* skull—nodded involuntarily as the movement inside his icy eyes intensified. The black specks vibrated at such a speed that the ice spheres melted outward from their cores. The surface of both spheres had been smooth and solid, but a crack appeared on the surface of one, then the other, then two more on the first, then four more on the second. On both spheres, lines and cracks linked with one another as the black specks moved quicker and faster, expanding their ranges.

Robert's teeth grinded together as the cracks increased, multiplying his vision, allowing him to see—for a fraction of a second—multiple versions of his stained skull. Some were marble, some were diamond, some were obsidian, some were emerald or ruby, but most were beyond description or comprehension. Soon the visions were no more than scurrying blurs. He had an urge to shut his eyes, but he had no lids. It didn't matter. A cloud of raspy sound enveloped his skull and shouted his name, shattering his eyes and freeing the blackness within.

4

———

Mr. Sailers's sudden entrance in the bathroom had caused him to pass out for several hours. When Robert woke up in the school nurse's office, she informed him he'd be allowed to go home for the rest of the day. He refused, insisting he was fine. The nurse then threatened to call his father at work to ask him to drop everything and immediately come pick up his son. That got Robert's blood up.

It was sixth period. Attendance in seventh period physics was the primary reason—maybe the only good reason—he'd even come to school. If he allowed himself to be sent home, he'd have to face his father in his angry I-told-you-so mode, and all the humiliation he'd endured in health class would have been for nothing.

After a heated argument, ending with him biting his tongue, he was able to negotiate a deal with the nurse. If she allowed him to attend his seventh-period class, he would go home immediately after it was over. They both agreed he would spend the remainder of the sixth period in the nurse's office under her watchful eye, though she took far more interest in an issue of *New High Times* than him.

Robert reclined on the bed staring at the dirty vanilla ceiling and its humming fluorescent lights, changing his position only to remove his sweater.

"Why is it so hot in here?"

"The thermostat is set at sixty-six degrees," the nurse said without looking up.

"Maybe someone turned it up?"

"I never move it," she said.

Robert returned to his back, gazing silently at the bright off-whiteness above. He felt more comfortable but was still very warm. He considered asking the nurse to take his temperature, but he really didn't want anything shoved into him. After his episode in the bathroom, his mouth and ears were still sensitive. Anyway, this woman seemed less than happy to do her job. He wondered, just briefly, if his mom were still alive and he were laying here in the same position, what would her attitude be? Would she spoil him as she did at home, or more acutely remember her mistake?

The bell rang. Robert grabbed his sweater and headed for the door. "Thanks."

"Here." The nurse gestured for him to come closer as he passed. "Take these if you feel nauseous again." She handed him a small clear bottle of pink capsules. "You don't need to take them with water."

"Great. Thanks." Robert stuffed the bottle into his left jeans pocket as soon as he was in the hall.

He'd hoped he was escaping a human-baking oven, but it was just as warm in the halls as it was in the nurse's office. At his locker, he tossed his sweater inside and took out the materials for the next class. Before shutting it, he closed his eyes and took a deep breath. Leigh was going to be in this class. It was the moment of truth. The time for an apology and a "So long, and good luck." His desk was right next to hers. Test or no test, it was impossible to avoid her. He prayed he could keep his nerves and thoughts straight to do this the right way. Last thing he needed was a repeat of their last meeting.

He slammed his locker and started down the hall, only to find himself face-to-face with Herman and the goddamned "Gutta-Step Crew."

"Yo, Goldnerd!" Herman grinned almost uncontrollably. "I knew it would finally happen—I *knew* it!"

Robert tried to maneuver his way around him. "Can't you stay away from me for just one day?"

"I can't, man, I can't. Not now...Not after I finally got my proof about you!"

"What are you talking about?" Robert narrowed his eyes as Herman's friends chortled.

"You! You finally got your first good look at some naked chicks and you couldn't take it! Runnin' out of classrooms, cryin', screamin', throwin' up all over the place...and those were only pictures! Now if you were confronted with the real thing...Ha ha ho boy, you'd be in *real* trouble!"

The Crew's boisterous laughing drew the attention of almost everyone in the hall.

"Dumb-ass zombies," Robert muttered as he again tried to get around them. They frustrated his attempts, moving to stay in front of him.

"Hey, it's understandable," Derrick said. "You choked on Thursday, and now it's finally being released, coming up and out!"

"Yeah," Jay said between coughs of laughter, "you feel better now? How do you feel now that you're not going to be able to roll around with other dudes in public for a while?"

"Great," Robert said. "Now I can go back to rolling around with your mother in private."

Jay's laughter stopped. "You prick, why don't you go—"

"Jump in your momma's bed?" Robert said. "In due time, at

the usual time and place. Don't be so anxious. Don't be like your momma."

Jay straightened his back, clenched his fists, and took a step forward. Jimmy put his hand to Jay's chest to hold him back as he announced a discovery.

"Look! The queer's even started paintin' his nails!"

He'd raised his free hand to pop Jay in his mouth, but Robert now gazed at it as the others stared. His nails were a deep shade of blue, verging on indigo. It didn't look like paint. The color was on the skin under the nails.

"Damn, man!" Derrick said. "Who does your nails? Sherrie at the beauty shop?"

"Yo, I guess that's your way," Herman said. "Most dudes would want to see her for somethin' else. You just go to get your nails done."

"Li'l Robbie boy blue..." Jimmy laughed. "Whose *horns* you been blowin'?"

Enough—he was going to be late. Finished with both talking and maneuvering, he walked straight toward the center of their grouping, intending to charge straight through them, and definitely ready to tussle if any refused to move.

"Watch it, fellas!" Herman said, quickly backing out of the way. "Don't let him get too close. You *know* where those hands have been!"

"Yeah," Derrick said, "he looks ready to *wrestle*! Don't let him get you in a crotch-clutch!"

They all backed away, clearing a path and guarding their groins as he passed. They hooted, hollered, and called after him, but Robert couldn't care less; he was glad they were out of his sight. They were far more obnoxious than ever before. Though Robert couldn't stand any of them, Herman was the only one who ever tried to instigate a verbal boxing match. In the past, Herman's shadows had chuckled at his remarks but otherwise left Robert alone. Yet another clique was evolving, or devolving, right before his eyes. Robert shook his head as he entered a side hall, then looked at his nails again.

Indigo, on both hands. He balled his left hand into a fist; his right-hand fingers curled around his textbook and notebook with the nails facing his right hip. They were out of sight for now, but how could he keep them hidden for the next hour? Would there even be any need?

No—the students in his physics class acted a lot more civilized than Herman's idiotic crew. He could count on that.

LEIGH, of course, wasn't her usual self. Brown jeans and orange sweatshirt, both looking one size too big for her. It was a style as dull as dishwater. She'd even taken the paint off of her nails and pinned up her hair as if she'd just joined the custodial crew. If not for the dress code, Robert figured she probably would've worn a kerchief. He wondered if this was her reaction to it being over between them. Even though they hadn't formally broken up, for her it was as good as over, and she was reflecting her post-breakup funk by looking terrible.

She was already in her seat when he'd entered the classroom, diligently reading through her notebook. He wanted to make eye contact; she would see the look in his eyes and that would trigger his apology and all that needed to follow for them to part ways amicably. But she didn't look up. She didn't make a sound, breathe irregularly, or react in any noticeable way as Robert walked by and took his seat next to her. She seemed completely engrossed in whatever she was reading. Robert didn't want to jerk her attention; her style of dress was a warning she might lash out if provoked by the slightest sound from him.

When class started, she raised her head and looked toward the front of the room, but she never turned in Robert's direction. He watched her out of the corner of his eyes, occasionally turning his head to the left just slightly. She didn't even flinch when Mr. Rawson announced to the relief of many that the anticipated test wouldn't be today. Her head seemed unable or unwilling to move right or left. It made Robert nervous. His jitteriness coupled with the classroom's mugginess made it difficult to concentrate, despite his great interest in the subject matter.

Mr. Rawson had begun with a discussion of the Greek goddess Iris and the Egyptian goddess Isis, drawing connections between the two before smoothly transitioning into the scientific properties of the rainbow. Normally Robert would've been on the edge of his seat. Today, the lecture sounded like so much prattle. This certainly wasn't due to the teacher's delivery. Even though this was the time of the day when most students and faculty yawned with every third breath, Mr. Rawson was running on a full tank, speaking as if fueled by something other than caffeine. His on-high style had its desired effect of keeping most students alert and interested. Robert tried his best.

"The rainbow is absolutely real," Mr. Rawson said, "but there seem to be some magical mysterious properties associated with it that even the most scientific individuals can't deny. For example, those great arching rainbows in the sky we've all seen...it is impossible to walk underneath them—"

"What if someone's walking at the speed of light?" Robert heard someone behind him mutter, followed by the sound of sniggering.

Mr. Rawson continued, apparently not hearing or unconcerned with the heckler. "This has caused some of the more mystical minded—or *misty*-minded—to speculate that these arches are doorways to other dimensions. And, as it is equally impossible to reach the legendary end of a rainbow, forget about finding a pot of anything there."

"Yeah," a student said, "you'll find that on Mr. Rawson."

Robert turned to see who'd inspired the stifled laughter this time. He shouldn't have been surprised to see it was Hank. The cutter smirked and blew a kiss at Robert as the latter turned away.

The teacher lectured on in his spaced-out manner, but the sight of Hank's gesture remained in Robert's mind as gusts of air blew on him every couple of minutes, as if oscillating electric fans sat on either side of him, pushing warm air instead of cool. No one else seemed bothered by the heat, even though everyone was wearing at least twice as many clothes as he. If he'd been at home, he would've stripped down further, to his underwear. Here, he just had to groan and try to bear it.

"Each water droplet up in those rainbows," Mr. Rawson said, "displays only one color at a time—at least to our eyes, just one color. A particular group of water droplets may display one color, say yellow, to you and another color, say green or blue, to a special loved one standing near you. Which colors the droplets display depends on the angle at which the viewer is observing each drop." He tugged at his bare ring finger as his eyes drifted toward the window. "Each drop is naturally colorless—like the gemstone you would give to a special loved one—but thanks to light and geometry, our eyes are treated to a breathtakingly beautiful light show phenomenon that's fit entertainment for the gods." A smile spread across his face, showing his pleasure at whatever pictures his words stirred in his own mind.

"Uh, excuse me, Mr. Rawson?"

"Hmm?" He shook his head to come out of himself. "Yes, Nathaniel?"

"I'm sorry," Nate said, "but there's been just too much religious talk for me in this class today. It's making me extremely uncomfortable."

"Yeah, me too," Hank said. "All this stuff about goddesses and love...it's making me *sick*. Please don't show us any pictures or I might have to throw up!"

Several students laughed, many of them glancing at Robert as he glared at Hank.

"All right, settle down everyone," Mr. Rawson said, the dreamy look on his face wiped clean away. "Please, let's continue."

The laughter and whispers didn't stop completely, but the teacher went on regardless. Robert took notes but noticed Leigh seemed to be sitting perfectly still, hands clasped on her desk, resting on her notebook. She sat with perfect posture and stared directly ahead. *Maybe she already knows all this stuff*, Robert thought, as he wiped sweat from his brow with his forearm. For the next several minutes, he kept his head down, writing furiously to take down every word Mr. Rawson said; he even accidentally copied down some of the smart-ass comments from other students. When his wrist began to hurt, he shook it and again glanced at Leigh. Her hands were still clasped, her eyes gazing at the front of the room. *What the hell is up with her?*

He turned his eyes downward and started to write again, but stopped, his attention drawn to the hairs on his forearm. The beads of sweat on them glistened, like morning dewdrops on black blades of grass. Oddly, the sweat didn't weigh them down. The hairs swayed and moved to the gusts of warm air—to which everyone but Robert seemed oblivious.

He moved his head up and down, left and right, staring at the beads. They weren't like the dewdrops, or even raindrops. No matter at what angle he viewed them, they continued to gleam green. "Blades of grass, indeed," he muttered.

"I'm sorry, Robert?" Mr. Rawson said.

He jerked his head up to find the teacher and much of the class looking at him.

Shit. Had they seen his sparkling forearms? Were they seeing green right now? He hurriedly wiped his hands across his forearms as he gaped at the teacher.

Mr. Rawson looked as confused as Robert felt, but after a moment, he asked, "Did you have the answer?"

"To what?" Missed opportunity. As soon as he said it, he knew he just should've said "no" and ended it.

"The question," Mr. Rawson said. Before Robert could even get a word out, the teacher continued, "If I were to say that the rainbow's colors are 'impure,' what do I mean by that?"

Robert shook his head slowly. He knew this, but his thoughts and tongue didn't want to cooperate. He swallowed a few times as a few sniggered around him. "It, uh, means...that the colors overlap...they're not distinct and defined with fine lines."

"Correct. The colors are pretty smeared." Mr. Rawson gave him an uncertain smile before shifting his gaze. "Now who here is able to give me a short description of the aspects of the secondary rainbow?"

Robert could have, if he'd wanted to. Now he wanted nothing more than all eyes off him. He wiped his hands and arms on his shirt as he cast a sideways glance at Leigh. She didn't show him the least bit of interest. That was good, if odd. He tried to forget about her and his skin as he concentrated on the class discussion.

"It's a result of two internal reflections in the water drops," Nate responded to the teacher, "as opposed to just one."

"The colors are opposite the primary bow," Hank added, "in reverse order. They go from red, orange, yellow, green, blue, to violet, from the center outward."

"While the primary bow is inverted," Nate said. "The colors proceed from blue to green and so on to red, outward from center."

"That's correct," Mr. Rawson said. "The colors of the secondary bow are perverted—"

"That's not the only colored thing in here that's perverted!"

Several students laughed as Mr. Rawson's brow furrowed. Hank's racist and homophobic comment seemed to knock him off his cloud, but left him at a loss for words. Robert was also at a loss. The assholes were out of line in more ways than one. Their barbs were usually nonvocal in the classroom; they saved their nasty comments for the halls and bathroom. And no one—certainly not them—had dared make a racist comment in the classroom within earshot of him, not since his junior high days.

Robert didn't move or speak, thinking maybe he'd misheard. But when Hank and Nate went on, culminating with Nate making a joke about goddesses Isis and Iris having lesbian sex while tying each other up in rainbows, it was Mr. Rawson who lost it as many students fell into hysterics.

"Class! *Class!*" The teacher's face grew beet-red as he stomped, futilely trying to retrieve the classroom from pandemonium.

Robert sat in silence, perplexed. Physics was one of his most advanced classes, filled with some of the school's brightest students. It had never before devolved into an unsupervised study hall. Did it have something to do with the unusual heat he'd felt?

He looked to his right and left. Leigh was the only one whose eyes didn't deviate from her open textbook. Robert couldn't tell if she was really reading or not; she wasn't turning any pages, or moving her fingers along the lines. She usually fought to answer the first questions Mr. Rawson tossed out, but she hadn't made a sound today. It had to be the heat. It was felt by others in the room, only they felt it in a different way. It was sparking unusual behavior, pushing people a few paces away from their usual selves.

Robert just tried to shut out the noise. He cast his eyes toward his desk, where his book lay, where his forearms lay. He blinked, looked closer, then blinked again at the glittering green hairs on his forearms. They were slithering across on his skin like living strings, tiny electrified snakes that snapped and crackled when they entered or emerged from his sweat pores. The muscles underneath the brown ground of his skin twitched, giving the whole scene the appearance of an unstable electric landscape.

The spectacle was both mesmerizing and frightening. But unlike the worms he imagined in his stomach, these didn't inspire nausea—for which he was thankful. He'd a feeling the pink capsules the nurse had given him wouldn't help his condition. But the fantastic sight inspired a thought. Was he witnessing a mere illusion, or was this something that could be categorized like the rainbow? *Real*, but—

The bell rang, breaking his hypnotic spell. He watched as the electric snakes slithered toward the nearest pores, entered, and stayed put. His forearms were now slick and hairless.

As students rushed for the door, he looked to his left. Leigh was gone. The class's biggest troublemakers were also gone. But Mr. Rawson's mood lingered.

"Quiz tomorrow!" he called. "Oral quiz on Thursday! And a written essay test on Friday!"

A few students stopped before running through the door, looking stunned. "On what?"

"You'll have to guess." Mr. Rawson turned his attention to the papers on his desk.

Robert collected his things, again feeling the warm sensations he'd felt during much of class. As he trudged toward the door, he wondered why he didn't feel so warm when he was watching the electric spectacle on his forearms.

"Robert?" The teacher's voice sounded like sandpaper.

"Yes, Mr. Rawson?"

"If...*when* you see Leigh, could you please tell her about the upcoming tests this week?"

Robert stared at him a moment. Why *her* specifically and not any of the others who were first out of the room? "Sure."

"Thanks, Robert." He leafed through papers on his desk as he spoke. "Maybe someday we can have a seventh-period session where everyone is in class *and* in their right minds."

Robert began to puzzle over his words, but it made his temples throb. As he left the room, he instead began to weigh whether he should go to wrestling practice or home. He'd made two promises on the latter, but now he had a lot of stress to work out. Just driving his beat-up 'Stang a few miles up and down some twisting dirt roads wouldn't do the trick.

He turned a corner to enter a side hall. Through the throng of students, at the far end, near one of the entrances to the gym, he saw Herman speaking with a girl in a pink-and-white outfit.

Leigh. It was unmistakable. She was dressed like her usual self—that polka-dotted pink bow in her hair clinched it—but how the hell had she changed clothes so quickly? And what the hell was she doing with Herman of all people? They were standing in proximity unusual for two individuals who hated each other.

Robert proceeded down the hall as if sleepwalking, never taking his eyes off of the pair as he maneuvered between others. The closer he got, the more it seemed the two were engaged in a happy conversation. When one was talking, the other smiled and listened. Robert wondered if he should interject. They just had to be talking about him; they had nothing else in common. He then considered whether he should just attempt to pass by unnoticed. He could easily turn around and reach his locker by another, more labyrinthine route. But he had to confront them. Now was no time to play the coward. He was on both of their shit lists at the moment and, for all he knew, they were devising some sort of revenge plot. If it turned out he was wrong, he could at least tell Leigh about the physics tests. And he could tell Herman to fuck off.

He approached now with more resolve, even pushing a few people out of his way. He didn't need anything slowing him down. He had tunnel-vision focus, but he noticed a blur fast approaching him from the left. He prepared to shove whomever it was. Student or teacher, he didn't give a shit; they were going to the wall or ground if it came to that. But instinct restrained him at the last moment.

"Hey, Goldner."

The blur's voice belonged to a friend. Reluctant to take his attention away from the scene of his disgust and mistrust, Robert responded as if he were being pulled from a dreamy nap back into reality.

"Uh, hey, Colin…What's up?"

"You tell me," he said. "That was a pretty interesting performance you put on last week."

"Yeah…" Robert couldn't completely turn away from the performance of the two mimes down the hall. Herman took both of Leigh's hands in his and simpered. Leigh simpered in return and brought her face closer to his.

"Yeah?" Colin sounded as if Robert had just stamped on his foot. "That's all you got to say? Where's the apology?" One word was enough to pull Robert's full attention.

"Apology?" he asked. "For what?"

"For embarrassing us, that's what!" His voice caused a few passersby to stop and watch, waiting for a fist or two to fly.

"You've got to be kidding me." Robert's eyes had narrowed at Herman and Leigh, but they now widened at Colin. He'd gone from disbelief in what he was seeing to greater disbelief in what he was hearing.

"I'm not laughing," Colin said. "You made us all look bad. What the hell's the matter with you? Don't you have any self-respect?"

"Did it ever occur to your stupid ass that I might be *sick*?" He was slow to anger with his friends, but who were his friends anymore? "I was in the hospital, you dumb shit."

"Yeah." Colin sneered. "First Davin, and then you, in a hospital bed. Probably the same one."

Robert swallowed his first response as he balled his right hand into a fist. Whether or not Colin saw it, he didn't back away; he only looked cockier, his upper lip curling like Elvis's. Maybe he didn't think Robert would hit him. Or maybe Colin thought a punch by a man who'd very recently spent some time in the hospital was nothing to fear. Most likely he'd just spotted his reinforcements coming down the hall.

"Hey, golden boy…"

Robert recognized the hillbilly's voice, but he didn't dare turn around. He wanted to keep his enemy-of-the-moment in full view.

No matter. Darren and Greg walked from behind and faced him as they flanked Colin. Duffel bags hanging from their shoulders, they were on their way to practice.

"Well, well, well, if it isn't jumpin' jackass flash!" Greg said. "You comin' to practice, Goldner?"

Robert kept his gladiator's gaze on Colin. "No."

"Why not?" Darren asked. "You quit the team without tellin' anyone?"

"No."

"Then what's the deal?" Darren said. "Don't care about us anymore? Now that you're out, we're out?"

"Yeah," Greg said, "you think just 'cause your season is over, and you ain't in it to win it anymore, then to hell with the rest of us?"

"That's *not* what I'm thinking." Robert ran his eyes over all of them, briefly—all too briefly—wishing he could make them flash like that girl at church.

He was in the mood to tussle, but fighting would be counter-productive, could even lead to a suspension. But wrestling them on the mat would serve the same purpose, teaching them a lesson and releasing some of his pent-up aggression. The only potential hazard was that many of his teammates would probably want to ensure he didn't escape a hellish punishment before leaving the room; Coach Myers would be cheering them on. If Robert got hurt, there'd be absolutely no sympathy, not even from his father.

"I'm thinking that maybe you *should* quit," Colin said. "We don't need your kind on the team anyway."

His kind…Robert clenched his teeth, debating whether he should he lay his text and notebook on the ground before engaging them, or just throw everything at one of them while charging at another. The inclination faded as he took a deep breath and replied to all three.

"I haven't quit, yet. And I'm *not* quitting now, no matter what you think. You assholes want to see me come to practice so badly, then fine. I'll be there."

"Fine, then," Greg said as he turned toward the gym. "You just better not try to pull any funny shit if we wrestle each other."

"Yeah," Darren grinned as he turned to follow, "stay away from *our* assholes! Maybe you better take a cold shower before practice."

Robert didn't bother to respond. Colin had no parting words either. He only scowled as he turned and followed the others toward the gym. Robert glared as they faded into the crosscurrents of students. Redneck, white hillbilly, and black rat. They were one target. He turned toward the other one.

Despite the flowing masses, he still had a fairly clear view of the mismatched couple near the gym's door. He now thought better than to approach them. In his mood, he could easily turn this bad scene into a worse one. Instead, he only watched as Leigh and Herman, still hand-in-hand, pulled closer to each other, and embraced.

It was impossible for Robert's heart to pump faster than it was already pumping, so his brain throbbed as if a second heart, pumping thoughts like blood at light-speed. All the thoughts coursing and crashing into one another made them incoherent. He couldn't understand when Herman's hands rubbed and squeezed Leigh's back as she massaged his in turn. It made no sense when their lips touched and locked for what seemed an eternity.

When they finally parted, both smiled broadly as Herman took Leigh by her hands and led her toward the nearby stairway. Robert lost sight of the couple when a small crowd of students strolled in front of them. When the crowd cleared, he saw no trace of either.

His brain kept throbbing, robbing him of good counsel on how to deal. The overriding urge in both body and mind was to go on a rampage, right now, taking out everyone he could get his hands on. Why not? His world had disintegrated. His father and friends dismissed him. Casual acquaintances mocked him. Enemies had grown into even bigger enemies. And the one person he could speak to, heart-to-heart, was locked away in a Heartland hospital, inaccessible to the public. Shit, for all he knew, Davin was already dead—all thanks to some big mystery.

Robert headed for the nearest exit to the parking lot. If he didn't remove himself from all human contact within the next few minutes, someone would die for sure.

PART III

ESTRANGED

1

———

Robert felt clearheaded by Tuesday morning. Despite Monday's events, he was determined to go to school to make a fresh start. First thing, he would break off his relationship with Leigh, whether or not she acknowledged his existence; at the end of first period, he would tell Coach Myers he was quitting the team; and for the rest of the day, if anyone had anything to say to him, he'd tune it out and smile. Most importantly, if he saw anything that bent the rules of reality, he wouldn't scratch his head; he'd just go with it. Everything one saw *wasn't* to be believed. He wasn't going to wait until Friday to resolve to become a new man. He'd start his birthday celebration three days early.

He joined his father for breakfast. Over maple and brown sugar oatmeal and fresh fruit, they discussed a vacation they might take over spring break. His muscles were a little sore, but Robert felt fine otherwise.

When his father left for work, he took a shower. As usual, he examined himself in the mirror after undressing. No rashes, blemishes, or anything resembling acne, just the same old scars he'd been carrying from season to season. He washed himself with a cloth, whistling some Coltrane all the while. It was only when he got out of the shower and stood in front of the mirror to dry himself that the whistling came to an abrupt end.

Silver specks were embedded in his skin, all over his body. They resembled tiny bits of metal, but they didn't hurt. At least not physically. The sudden sight of them inflicted a psychic pain. Rather than dry off completely, Robert bolted into his room to get dressed quickly, putting the sight out of his mind just as quickly. But he was damned by the confluence of interior design and Mother Nature as he stepped into the patch of light between his window and dresser.

The open blinds allowed the morning sun's rays to stream through while the mirror above his dresser reflected the rising sun's splendor. Robert's body was caught between; he only managed to put on his boxer shorts before suddenly feeling like the Tin Man from Oz. He screamed as his skin tightened, but no one heard. In his final moments of mobility, he shut the window blinds and bedroom door, and he unplugged or depowered everything that could be plugged in or run with batteries. He knew his physics. Whatever was out to get him, it drank the nectar of electromagnetism. He used his last little bit of mobility to lie on his bed.

His muscles burned. His joints cracked and popped. Once he'd gotten to his back and stretched out his legs, he found he could no longer move without feeling as if his muscles would tear or his bones would break. The glittering specks in his skin felt like sharp pieces of metal, poking, stabbing, and sticking deeper into his flesh each time he flexed, twisted, turned, or shifted a part of his body. He finally lay still, like a corpse.

He couldn't move, but he could think, and one thought took precedence: He was almost completely lost to himself. The events of the past two weeks had proven that.

This was his life. Not a Born Loser, but a Born Mistake who learned the meaning of life early: It's nothing but pain and suffering in a world of illusions. Maybe that was the Big Mistake of his being—he saw things too clearly too early. He wondered why there weren't more suicides. Hell, maybe those who had discovered Life's Lesson, like he just had, intuitively realized things got worse after suicide, so they go on and bear the misery here. Just like Robert had resigned himself to gazing at his skin—sprinkled with silver glitter, sparkling from black to red to orange to yellow to green to blue to indigo to violet and then briefly to silver before going back to black again. The circular journey through the visible light spectrum was unending, and each piece of glitter went through the color-cycle at its own pace.

Robert only glanced at the twinkling spots and laughed. His thoughts spun around to play in his brain's various shadowed regions. Dementia was no longer at bay.

In the dark room, his body provided the room's primary source of light. It even provided a sound: a murmuring purr similar to an electric hum, originating from deep within his chest. On his bed he lay, stiff as wood, gazing dumbly at his glistening self, hardly listening to his heartbeat or his breathing. This is how he would go out, like a lazily decorated Christmas tree, boasting plenty of pretty lights but excluding everything else, even the pine needles—though he certainly felt needles pricking on and under his skin. He wondered what Jesus would think about all this.

Robert's blasphemous thoughts tripped from light to light, proceeding in multiple directions at once, enhancing the electric hum as they went. These thoughts were threading, sewing, knitting, and stitching new and bizarre connections with his body. His subconscious mind was altering the *matter* of himself. The realization of it was enough to push him to the brink of total insanity. He needed to rethink things. He needed to come up with metaphors and link them in a coherent narrative in order to stay relatively sane.

He thought of forests. The forest of the mind. And ponds.

Memory ponds. He focused on one such pond in the forest of his mind...but he lost control of the story as soon as it began.

Strange-limbed creatures crawled out of the plasmic memory pond. Hundreds, then thousands, then millions of them, all resembling mutated ants. They crawled out faster and faster in every direction as Robert's body seemed to rot, rapidly decomposing from hard and sturdy wood into a mass of brown sugar. The intangible mutated ant-creatures became tangible as they scurried beneath his skin then poured out to the surface. The hurrying ants picked up the sparkling pieces of glitter and carried them as they tunneled in and out of the needle-thin holes in the brown sugary sand of Robert's flesh. The lights now moved in patterns across his skin. These creatures from memory were up to no good.

Robert closed his eyes and concentrated, trying to come up with new metaphors and form a new narrative, a new song of himself. He couldn't let the rebel thoughts win.

For a moment, nothing happened. Then his brain contracted, as if his skull were in a vise. He opened his eyes, ready to scream, but the pain left as quickly as it came. He looked again at his body, at the lights, then the pain came again, squeezing for twice as long. This time, he didn't want to scream. The pain ceased, then came again—this third time, it didn't stop. The pressure on his brain all but blinded Robert as his body shuddered, loosening the brown sugar, shaking it down.

The ants ran in a frenzy as Robert shook uncontrollably, disintegrating himself, as a spiderweb of lightening shot across his body and his consciousness blinked him out of space and time.

ROBERT'S CONSCIOUSNESS eventually pushed him back into the

present. Whatever "present" this was. How many hours—or days —had passed?

He stared at his bedroom ceiling. It reflected his image back to him like a magnifying mirror. His skin was no longer flesh, or wood, or brown sugar. While he was unconscious, it had transmuted into glass that magnified whatever was under it. He could now see into himself all too well—and what he saw was an orange-red sludge. Tomato soup had taken the place of his blood, bones, and organs.

He still wasn't able to turn over. His glass skin was rigid, unyielding. And it was no use to shut his eyes; he could see clear through his eyelids. He was, however, able to allow his mind to drift, resulting in a willed blindness.

He wondered if, by the laws of natural science, the double magnification of the mirror and his skin should make everything appear blurry instead of giving him a superclose and detailed reflection of himself. Had Mr. Rawson ever discussed this? *With my luck, he's discussing it today, whatever day this is.*

It wasn't unusual for his skin to feel itchy, especially when he'd neglected to apply lotion after showering. But how could glass feel itchy? Robert did away with the willed blindness and concentrated harder, *looked* closer, until, as he'd guessed, he saw something moving on his new skin. Tiny crystalline creatures, some yellow, some blue, some green, some black, but most of them colorless. It took him another moment to realize just what they were doing.

They skated fast and slow, in straight lines and in wavy lines. Some darted across his skin at long distances in no discernible pattern, as if simply on a mission to get from one point to another. Some kept retracing their skate-lines, moving back and forth, or in circles. All of them were scratching the surface, digging furrows into the surface, trying to break *through* the surface.

Robert was nauseous. The tomato-soup substance within him

was coming to a boil. In time, it may've melted the glass from within. Whatever the promise, the process wasn't silent. Throughout his entire body, the substance was a sea storm of red and black noise. He would've dragged his body into the bathroom, but in immovable glass skin, all he could do was look on and despair.

He gazed at the bubbling substance pressing against the glass, each bubble harboring several black specks within it. Without much effort, his eyesight sharpened and he clearly saw each black speck as a mass of hundreds of blue specks—further, each blue speck was comprised of thousands more, each an alien color, unnameable. Pulling back, he counted thousands of transparent bubbles under his skin and wondered how many more there were he couldn't see. He suspected the bubble-globes contained populations of something more fundamental than atoms.

Maybe his life wasn't a Big Mistake. Maybe his body was a one-man universe of...something. Maybe there was big meaning within this.

Or maybe there wasn't. Maybe this was all part of the world of illusion in which the so-called "living" were trapped. Maybe he just happened to be living life to the fullest. Maybe the diamond-creatures' mission was to empty him out.

His thoughts were flying amuck, incoherently weaving through various times and places. But he thought he at least now understood the noise within him. It was a composition, either composing or decomposing *him*. Another song of himself. Each black speck and blue speck and alien speck in the bubbles was a note of music comprising the essential parts of his being. In the end, it wouldn't be ashes to ashes, dust to dust; for him, it would be bubble to bubble, note to note.

But who would hear?

His glass shell cracked and shattered as his consciousness wiped him clean from the here-and-now.

Robert heard a low rumbling coming from the other side of his closed bedroom door. He opened his eyes to see the door itself tremble while the floorboards beneath the carpet outside it creaked.

He didn't know how much time had passed since he'd last lost consciousness, but he did know something else was in the house with him. Not his dad. The creaking didn't match his gait. The sounds didn't even match any normal pattern of human footfalls —not walking, running, or skipping.

Whatever may've been outside, it seemed some kind of spirits possessed the walls inside his bedroom. The walls and ceiling looked like ponds on a breezy day, the waters dyed red, green, yellow...every variety of apple. He started to wonder why he'd thought of apples but stopped when the undulations ceased and the noises in the hall fell silent.

Calm before the next song, he thought. His muscles were no longer sore. His joints were no longer rigid. But he wasn't eager to move. Mentally, he just wasn't there yet. So he remained comfortably numb, not even flinching when his door opened and she walked in.

"What witch's fruit did *you* eat?" she asked with a smile conveying deep concern mixed with mild amusement.

The blonde wore electric-blue pants and gloves, gray boots, and a black scarf with intricate indigo designs. She walked to the side of the bed with far more grace than usual, gazing into his eyes all the while.

Robert hiccupped.

She sat on the bed's edge and bent her face closer, parting her lips. Even as he kept hiccupping, she said nothing, just breathed. The pattern of Robert's breathing changed. Soon, his exhalations matched her inhalations. His breathing steadied as cold breath wisped from between her lips and past his, the condensation touching the tip of his warm tongue. A tingling spread throughout his body, rejuvenating his ability to see, think, and speak in the present.

"*Leigh?*" he managed after a sneeze. "What are you doing here?"

"Obviously, I'm worried about you. Why else would I be here?"

"But...how'd you get in? Is my dad home? What time is it? What day—"

"*Shush.*" She put her forefinger on his lower lip. "Just relax. Your dad isn't here. I'm guessing he's at work, like you and I should be at school. You skipped yesterday and I heard you were skipping today, thanks to some wicked sickness...I just wanted to see how you were doing. I would've brought tomato soup or something, but I didn't think about it until I got here."

He tried to sit up, but a cramp in his gut kept him in place. The girl smiled as if, despite their recent troubles, despite him never apologizing, she'd already forgiven him and they were already friends again. Then her expression changed.

"Good lord"—she stood up, rubbing her arms in spite of her long sleeves—"no *wonder* you're sick. It's freezing in here! And you're just lying around in your shorts! Are you sick in the head, too?"

The entire house was probably freezing. Why was she just now noticing? "I feel fine. Not cold or hot."

"Let me feel." He clenched his teeth and tried to bury his head in the pillow. It felt like a sheet of ice had landed on his forehead, but her hand quickly warmed to match his temperature. "Not really a fever, I guess. Still, I'm going to turn the heat up." She walked into the hall, closing the door behind her.

He heard the door close, but nothing beyond that. No footsteps, no creaking floorboards, no brushing against the walls. Only a long moment of silence. He then heard air rushing through the vents so forcefully it almost made him jump. The house hummed so loudly he didn't even hear his bedroom door reopening.

It swung open all the way, but no one came through. Instead, a fogged-up window took up the entire space of the doorframe. Robert gazed at it, fearing he was descending into delirium again, and fearing more for Leigh's safety if she came to his side as he was freaking out.

He swung his legs over the side of the bed and stood with trepidation. He took two steps toward the fogged doorway as the steam evaporated. The window's glass was warped. A wrinkled, silver-metallic foil was on the other side of it. In between glass and foil, a shadow materialized, matching Robert's height and outline. He blinked when the shadow stepped forward, taking on greater dimensions. The glass cracked and dissolved as she passed through, her face taking on greater detail. Robert took two steps backward, almost tripping as the girl approached, smiling crookedly, her teeth like stained-glass shards.

"Artemisia?" Robert stood his ground, though his knees felt like jelly.

The girl cocked her head as her brow furrowed. "Who?"

Robert blinked as if someone were shining penlights into his eyes. After a moment, he could see clearly, and he found himself looking at Leigh. She was now wearing silver gloves and boots, blue jeans and a black turtleneck, and a snakeskin scarf. The doorway behind her was clear.

"Leigh?"

"Yes, '*Leigh*,'" the girl said. "Who the hell else is it supposed to be?"

"I...you looked like...No one."

She gave him a look that he remembered from their last argument, like she wanted to punch him in the chin. Instead she turned away and unwrapped her scarf. "You know, you don't have to hide anything from me anymore." She laid the scarf on his desk chair and turned back to him, her eyes softening. "After all this time, all we've been through, it doesn't make sense." She moved closer. "No more secret gardens, hmm?"

Robert couldn't help but look into her eyes as she spoke. Their shape seemed off, as if for the first time he saw hints of Asian ancestry. Her irises were definitely not the bluish gray they were supposed to be but a wavy mixture of forest green and pumpkin orange. Beyond them, in the blackness of the pupils, he thought he saw something flickering. He knew he was hallucinating again—he just had to be—but some of what he was seeing and hearing was real. He just wasn't sure how much.

She was no more than two feet in front of him. Robert leaned his head forward an inch and tried to focus in on those eyes. She leaned closer as well, smiling, as if about to divulge an amusing secret. Those flaming wisps, they seemed so real. He was about to ask about them, but without warning, she shut them, grabbed his arms and pulled him closer.

Together, we're a lie...

It didn't start off as a romantic kiss; it felt as if it had been initiated out of panic. But as their lips remained touching, and after he let his eyes close, the kissing became more relaxed, then rose in passion as he let an almost forgotten habit have its way. His heartbeat increased; his lips throbbed like two pulses. *Time, untie me.* Before drawing her face away from his, she clamped both of her lips onto his bottom one. He felt a sharp pinch.

"What's the matter?" she asked, her eyes still shut.

"I think you bit me." He put his index finger on his lip.

"Sorry." She stepped back, her eyelids gradually parting. "I guess I just couldn't control myself."

"Why are you kissing me anyway?" The stuff on his finger didn't look like blood, just viscid saliva. It tasted a little like grape jelly. "We're no longer together, remember?"

"I remember." Her eyes dulled. "Remembering is the reason I'm here."

He cocked his head as she lazily turned away from him,

looking toward the window.

"We need more light in here," she said, "Do you mind if I open the shades?"

"Yeah, I do." He remembered what began the latest major attack on his senses. "How about just turning on the lamp instead?" He gestured toward the lamp as he went to check his lip in the mirror. She clicked it on, and Robert got a better view of his face. There was no blood; the skin wasn't even broken. Everything seemed normal.

"You're mistaken."

She came up behind him, resting her chin on his left shoulder, looking at his image in the mirror. He didn't say anything as he looked at her face's image. It was radiant. The right side of his face reflected the lamplight shining on it, but her face seemed to glow even brighter than the lampshade. He wondered about the light source as he focused on her eyes. Two eggshell ovals centered with circles of black coal. Her pupils appeared dilated to the absurd point where her irises were too thin to be seen.

"Mistaken?" he whispered.

"I don't bite." She frowned. "Unless it counts."

Robert turned from the mirror and looked at her directly. Her face was darker than the mirror image. She wasn't frowning, but smiling. And her eyes were as normal as could be, if a little bloodshot.

"Come here." She grabbed his hand and led him to the bed. "Let's sit and talk."

She sat down on the bed's edge and pulled him down next to her. He was reluctant, but found her grip unusually tight, her tug unusually strong. Once seated, she held onto his left hand with both of hers, staring down at it. She didn't really seem interested in speaking, so Robert filled the silence.

"You know, I never got the chance to apologize," he said. "We'd been together for so long, I didn't want to end it like we ended it."

"It's not over yet." Her eyes remained downcast. It was almost as if she were praying. With her clasping his hand the way she was, it was like she was praying for him.

"We should remain friends," Robert said. "We've had a lot of good times together."

"We have," she muttered. "How many of them do you remember?" There was a definite change in her voice. It had a tinge of bitterness, as if some bad memories had welled up in her head. Robert tried to conjure up a few good memories, quick.

"Do you remember," she said, "the time we met in the park in Baltimore and I stopped your heart? Or the time we met in Dupont Circle and I gave you an aneurysm?"

Her head rose and her face turned toward him. Robert sat transfixed at the crooked smile of Artemisia, staring at him now with flickering orange-green eyes, both of them unquestionably sheltering flames. He gasped as the lamplight clicked off. He had no words, just the creeping realization that his hand was being squeezed, tighter and tighter, as a sensation of cold crawled up his arm.

"Hello again," she whispered, bringing her face closer to his. He felt paralyzed. Either the shock of Leigh's sudden transformation into Artemisia or the icy vise-grip on his hand prevented him from resisting. He didn't close his eyes, but his vision blurred, making everything in sight blend together. When their lips touched, parts of him pulsed—his lips, his toes, his fingers, his ears, his cheeks, his biceps, his thighs—as if he'd sprouted tiny hearts all over his body.

Time, untie me...

She pulled her lips away as his vision again focused on the broken-glass smile spreading under her flickering orange-green eyes. She was now dressed in orange and black.

"*God,*" he muttered. "What in hell?"

"There is no Hell for you," the girl said. "There's just me."

He'd truly gone beyond mad. He was trapped in some kind of

inescapable, shifting realm that refused to give any consistency to his experiences. It was like a horrific and extremely vivid dream, similar to the ones he got when pumped up with medicine, recovering from a cold. Whatever afflicted him now was worse than a cold; he was on his deathbed, and the result was a fusion of reality and fantasy.

Don't quit, damn it.

He wouldn't. He wouldn't commit suicide. If he did, he was sure he'd be in for something worse. The only thing he would do was take control over whatever part of what he was experiencing was imaginary.

"Leigh..." He used every bit of concentration and will within to make the girl retake the appearance of his ex-girlfriend.

"Sorry, junior," she said. "It won't work. I'm here now. *Completely.*"

Robert tried harder, even squeezing his eyes shut. "*Leigh...*"

"No Leigh. Only me." She released his hand and took her weight off the bed. Robert opened his eyes to see her opening the window blinds. Three ravens and one dove sat on the windowsill on the other side of the glass. One by one, they flew out of sight, as if fleeing from his gaze. The girl walked back to the bed and stood in front of him. Looking up at her, he realized that she was taller than before. She was approaching seven feet.

He swallowed. "If this is real...hell, even if it isn't, can you please tell me what the fuck is happening here?"

"Right now, I am." She smirked, pleased with a joke he didn't quite get.

"What happened to Leigh? Where is she?"

"Out of the picture," Artemisia said. "Seems she had a little mishap not too long ago and had to be taken to the hospital."

He'd the sudden urge to spring up and confront this woman not-so-subtly implying she'd hurt Leigh. But he had no idea of what he was dealing with. His legs twitched, but he remained seated.

Artemisia seemed to sense his frustration and smiled at it. "You may not completely remember me yet, so allow me to reintroduce myself. I am Artemisia, heir of Lilith."

"Who?"

"You'll please excuse all the changes in appearance and whatnot. My mind is constantly ticking through alternate space-times, multiple dimensions, all of them closely related"—the flames in her pupils flared—"just as you and I are. I have to concentrate to remain stable, and it was touch and go for a while there. You seem to be giving off an unusual amount of...energy today. In such close proximity, it was a bit harder for me to control what I was saying and doing as I shook myself in to where I needed to be. But don't worry, I'm completely *here* now. And after I carry out my mission in the name of my true mother and her cousin, you won't be."

He felt light-headed as he listened to this woman standing over him, talking strangely, threatening him. He needed a firmer grip.

"We met—we *first* met—at church?"

"Not our first meeting," she said. "But I was at the church mostly in body, not mind."

Robert narrowed his eyes. "What are you?"

"The same thing you are. The world once called and will soon again call us saints, angels, demons, prophets, giants...whatever. It doesn't matter. By the grace of my spiritual mother, I have seen the deepest levels of Reality. I know—as you really do—that God, our Creator, has gone insane. The dimensions are collapsing. We've come a long way from Paradise, and soon, a Most High 'son of Adam' will rise to make sure we never return, that all is plunged into chaos."

His mind was cloudy, but he could still put two and two together. "And you think I'm this 'son of Adam'?"

"You will be. A piece of Adam's soul is mixed with yours." Her eyes flashed again. "We've met many times before, you always in different bodies under different names, and me...well, I have a psychic link with you, all of *you*, all of the keepers of Adam's pieces; the mazes of our consciousness crisscross each other, like a hyperdimensional chessboard. I've been tracking you—Robert Omari Goldner—for a few days. Sometimes invisible, sometimes as myself, sometimes in multiple states of being at once. Each time in the past, when I found a keeper of Adam's soul bits, I did my duty and walked away the victor, but everything remained spoiled. Turns out I've just been taking out random sons. The world will be engulfed in anarchy unless I stop the strongest, most powerful son."

Was he expected to believe this? Could he believe it, in light of the past several days? "Am I...am I really sick?"

"Self-righteous and self-hating. A bundle of dangerous contradictions. You show all the signs. Ever wondered why you're so good at abstract thinking? Math, for instance? And even poetry, when you've the guts to admit it?"

Of course he never wondered. Different people had different talents. But what talents he discovered in himself, he'd worked hard to develop. "I read, and I think about what I read."

"Your mind," she said, "when it's free, relaxed, can travel between spaces and times, making connections unseen and unconsidered by those constrained to surface matters, those focused on the literal. Surely you've experienced this. Eden's rejected seeds managed to get buried under the skin of some folks. *That's* your sickness. And mine. What's more, it's a sign of the crimes against Lilith and Eve."

He knew the names. "Bible myths," he mumbled.

"Much more than that," she said. "In the reigning tradition of this land, Adam and Eve happily created humanity. But there's a deeper, more accurate story. Adam and his first wife were created together—at the same time, of the same matter, and in the same space—but she separated from him, ran to the wilds of another dimension, because she—Lilith—didn't want to submit to his macho bullshit. God gave Adam a second wife, made from a piece of Adam, his rib. Not as strong as Lilith, Eve was willing to be somewhat submissive. But she still had a mind of her own. In fact, she wanted to develop it to its utmost potential. By doing so, by stepping out of her place, tasting this forbidden fruit of Knowledge and—mistake—trying to share the gift with her dimwitted partner, she was damned, blamed by all humans to follow—even the women—as being the gateway for Hell on Earth. All for trying to know good and evil, trying to *truly* know the Creator, a creator whose spark of insanity began when humankind was created."

Robert remembered his runaway hallucination in the church parking lot. Had Artemisia in some way inspired it?

"For her actions, Eve was ultimately sacrificed by partisans of Adam. The family of Cain slaughtered her like an animal, cut her up into bits and pieces. Lilith gathered these pieces and planted them in another dimension, a Ground that will be the foundation of the harmonious world to come—a new, universal Garden of Paradise—unless Adam's followers have their way. In their zealotry, his followers sacrificed him as well. But they didn't bother with the body; they extracted the soul, worked a little *magick* on it, divided it, so that its pieces also worked as seeds, planted deep in the souls of a select few in this dimension. Any of this ringing a bell?"

Robert shook his head. "Just stories. I've heard hundreds." Though the last part was certainly new to him.

"Some stories are truer than others. As you know, stories that are *truly* believed help create Reality."

No, he didn't know. Or at least he wasn't sure about all that she was saying. Robert gazed at the giant of a woman standing over him. It seemed she had grown a few inches taller while speaking.

"I know your biological father's name is not Adam," she said, "as my biological mother's name is not Lilith. But those who believe—*truly* believe—in the popular story of Adam and Eve rule the world today. They've ruled the world during its most crucial moments of development. And those who've sided with Adam and his sons have always held sway, turning our world into the mess it's become—bigotries, perpetual war, disease, slavery—proving Adam was the true gateway to Hell on Earth. But the world is at a tipping point. Universal bedlam, eternal chaos, cosmic muck—all the worst outcomes lead back to *you.*"

"Listen," Robert said. "Whatever you're crusading against, I haven't had anything to do with it. I *won't* have anything to do with it."

"My mind has flipped through pasts, presents, and futures," she said. "Sometimes simultaneously, like watching a hundred different movies at the same time. I know you can relate to that... cousin. Not knowing when or where you are. Honestly, all people can relate, to an extent. But with us, it has a greater effect on our surroundings. And it becomes more pronounced the closer we get to maturity."

It hit him like a brick. What he'd seen earlier—the appearance of "Leigh" in his room and her nonsensical talk—he was then witnessing this "flipping through" from the other side. He wondered what the people around him had seen and heard as he flipped through over the past several days. Whatever, it had certainly helped twist his name and reputation—but to what extent? His perceptions of others—their words and actions—had undoubtedly been distorted at times. How much of what he'd heard and seen over the past two weeks was *real?*

Well, whatever was or wasn't, he refused to swallow most of what Artemisia was now trying to feed him.

"I've been fortunate enough to stop all the sons of Adam I've encountered before they've reached their prime," Artemisia said. "I've seen many variations of past, present, and future—but I've also finally pinpointed one certainty. The son of Adam I'm looking for—the Most High—has your biological mother's blood running through his veins."

Enough. Whatever the hell else was going on, he'd be damned if he'd let another use his mother's name in vain. Robert began to stand.

Artemisia grabbed him by the throat with her left hand, her thumb on his Adam's apple, choking him as she lifted him off his feet.

She was more than seven feet tall at this point. With one arm, she'd lifted him a head above her; his dangling feet didn't even scrape the floor. Her grip tightened. He'd once held his breath underwater for about ninety seconds; he figured that's the amount of time he had to get free.

"Take a good look," she said. "Remember me, yet?"

Her eyes glowed as she showed off that stained broken-glass smile. He dug all his fingernails into her forearm, but her turtle-neck's sleeve was impenetrable. He kicked at her legs and thighs, but it was like kicking a brick. His fingers tried to pry hers away, but her fingers may as well have been under his skin.

He figured he'd less than thirty seconds before she choked the life out of him. He was down to desperate maneuvers. He couldn't bite her. His hands and feet were useless. All he could do was look at her.

He opened his eyes as wide as he could and gazed into hers, not knowing what he would do, but trusting it all to his survival instinct. Light from the window streamed into his pupils like a faucet filling a cup. What began as a stream became a flood until all he could see was a fluorescent yellow-blue stew, dotted with black specks. He then released it. It felt as if acid were running over his eyelids as his pupils vomited all they'd taken in. He saw only a yellow-blue flash as he heard a shriek and the fingers loos-ened from his throat.

Robert dropped to his feet and fell back onto the bed. He'd hurt her. He'd stopped her from choking his life away—but only momentarily. Before he could even sit up, she rushed at him, grabbed his shoulders and pinned him down. She straddled his hips and brought her face down closer to his. Her eyes flickered with that orange-green glow, now strong enough to light up half of the room. Her jack-o'-lantern smile also returned. Robert was no longer intimidated.

"I'm going to bite your damn throat out," she said.

He didn't give a shit about her threats or the reasons behind them. He looked into her eyes and tried not to blink as he looked deeper—within her and himself simultaneously. His eyelids shivered as he imagined a cold wind blowing over the candle flames of her eyes. The flames shuddered and quelled, but they didn't go out completely. Whatever invisible wicks supported her little fires reduced to a dark red glow. Her irises faded to a deep aqua then dark forest green before finally settling on a coffee brown, presumably her eyes' natural color.

"What do you think about—"

His triumphant quip was cut short when her eyes flared with new colors, and new intensity. The flames now flickered and shifted between a pale violet and a bright blue. Under her rock-like hands, his shoulders felt like knobs of ice, interfering with the signals between his brain and arms. His legs felt just as useless with the mountain of her body on his hips.

Artemisia opened her mouth wide, giving full display to her stained broken-glass teeth. They'd have no difficulty chewing out his throat.

He cursed her, but she shushed him by blowing a cloud of condensed air sprinkled with sparkles. It obscured his vision as he had the impression of someone slapping a mask of ice onto his face. Frisson shot through his body as his eyes rolled up into his head.

"In the name of Eve," she said. "Bite for bite…"

Robert's brain quivered as he saw and *felt* cyan, heard a piercing wail, then experienced nothing more.

2

Psychic bolts of lightning. That was the best explanation. The electrical activity of his brain and nervous system had somehow amped up to such a degree as to shock the hell out of his bedroom invader. After all, if she was to be believed, they shared the same brain patterns and all.

Whatever the trick, he woke up later that evening to find all traces of Artemisia long gone and his body feeling better than it had in weeks. He immediately called Leigh, left a message on her cell, then took a shower without incident. When his father came home from work, he said Robert looked like a new man. Robert sidestepped any mention of what had happened and simply thanked his father for the care he'd given him. The two had an enjoyable dinner and afterward Robert had one of the best sleeps of his life.

On Thursday morning, he woke up feeling a little heavy in the head, but otherwise fine. Regardless, his father refused to let him attend school. Robert spent the morning listening to mellow jazz while ruminating on all the mysteries of the past week. Leigh hadn't called him back, so he knew something had certainly happened to her. He weighed the idea of cold-calling her parents to check on her status, but he knew that would end badly. He also considered calling Dr. Wright to inquire about Artemisia, but he couldn't imagine any kind of conversation that wouldn't prompt Miss PhD to storm over to finish what her niece had started. There was just no diplomatic way to convey, "Your niece is probably some kind of demonic witch and she definitely tried to kill me." He still didn't know what, if anything, he should say to his father, but he figured some epiphany would strike him on Sunday, if Artemisia dared to show up at church.

He did, however, make one phone call. Davin's mom was at work so he was forced to leave a message. He apologized, sincerely and profusely, for anything he might've done to contribute to Davin's condition. He then begged her to call him back—not his father—for a status update. When speaking to her, he'd try to convince her to somehow sneak him in to the HSA hospital where Davin was, hopefully, recovering.

Robert spent the rest of the day perusing books on physics and mathematical theories, pausing every thirty minutes or so to give thanks that the day was moving along without unwelcome visitations, from without or within.

On Friday morning, after yet another good night's rest, his father again refused to let him attend school. Robert felt even better this day than the day before, but he didn't argue. It was his birthday after all. And he knew the first day he returned to school, Mr. Rawson would have him stay late to take all the tests and quizzes he'd missed. That was no way to celebrate turning seventeen. He'd worry about the exams on Monday. He'd much rather spend this day—the sixth anniversary of his mother's death—in meditation.

But sitting in a dark room wasn't his way. Neither were long, solitary walks in nature. He had to get his heart pumping, his muscles moving. So he put on his winter running gear, grabbed his MP3 player and spare house key, and walked out onto the patio.

Even under the early morning's pallid sky, warmth flushed through his body. Everything in sight was under a thin layer of snow or frost, yet he was overwhelmed in both a running jacket and a sweatshirt. He went back inside and stripped down to a sleeveless T-shirt. When he left the house next, the chilled air was invigorating.

He ran through a neighbor's yard, crossed a street, and entered the woods by one of its many jogging trails, completely free of snow or ice. He was thankful he could keep a decent pace without having to think about where he was stepping. He wanted to think about nothing but his mom—*good* memories and the possibilities of an afterlife. He could only slip into that meditative state once his breathing, his heartbeat, and the thudding of his shoes combined to make a music that enhanced what he heard on his player.

He wound his way through the woods, going wherever the paths took him. Through the gaps in the trees, he occasionally caught glimpses of side streets and other peoples' houses, but he mostly saw trees, with their frost-covered branches, icicles, and straggling brown leaves.

His body felt good. Each breath exchange with the cold breeze seemed to purify all of his inner recesses, and the fresh air against his exposed skin felt wonderful. He was even building up a sweat. *Another incentive to keep moving at a good pace*, he thought. *Unless I want the sweat to turn to ice.*

He'd run for half an hour, comparing the first ten years of his life to the last seven, when a tingling ran over his exposed skin. Each hair on his face and arms felt like a burning wick, each hair follicle felt clogged with ice. The tingling moved on, deeper into his skin and muscles, seeming to penetrate his bones. There was nothing on his forearms. He figured the sensation was just the result of being active after several days of relative inertia. He ran for several minutes more, then smelled something pungent. Some kind of rotting fruit. He looked to either side of him. There wasn't any fruit—just gnats.

He swatted at the black specks hovering around him, drawn to his head and arms, and sped up. He didn't lose them, so he tried to outmaneuver them, sprinting down a path and then turning at a right angle to sprint down an intersecting path, or sprinting one direction and then suddenly turning one hundred eighty degrees to sprint in the opposite direction. Nothing worked. If anything, the specks' numbers multiplied.

Both his heart rate and breathing seemed at their limits. Sweat drenched him, but his skin felt neither warm nor cool. That wasn't normal. Without breaking his stride, Robert looked at his palm, and saw straight through to the bone. Instinctively, he curled his fingers. His palm felt like thick jelly. He slowed to a trot. All of his skin had the texture of the strange jelly. He stretched his arms in front of him and shook them. In both sensation and appearance, the flesh wobbled like Jell-O. Robert stopped running altogether, and hordes of black specks and blue spots descended on his arms and face.

Robert sprinted as fast as he could manage. The gnats left him, but they were close behind. He decided he'd just run as fast as he could until he got home. He spotted a clearing up ahead and tried to run even faster. He'd figure out how far he was from home once he got into wide-open space. But emerging from the woods, he didn't get much further than five steps when he saw the rising sun in its full glory.

Transfixed, he saw the thick shafts of winter sunlight splinter into needle-thin rays before entering his eyes, his face, his arms, and his hands. Robert screamed himself silent as the rays' electromagnetic needles sewed in and out of his pores, stitching his entire body to the atoms in the surrounding environment. He couldn't make a sound as his quivering body rose several feet into the air. He dropped his MP3 player, the earbuds jerking out of his head as it fell. He still couldn't hear a thing. His vision, however, was far too clear.

With his head tilted back, he saw a streak of red lightning split the middle of the deep blue sky, leaving a purple crack in the Earth's false ceiling.

Its stitching process complete, the sun played with its new marionette, using the light-strings attached to his body to stretch and bend his arms, placing his hands on the top of his tilted head. Unable to blink, his eyes gazed at the sky's purple crack as it widened.

Violet seeped from the crack and bled in streaks across the sky. Robert's fingers arched; his fingernails dug into the centerline of his scalp. The sky's crack broadened as his fingers dug deeper, puncturing his skull. He felt no pain, only awe as the bloodied sheet of sky above ripped, pried open like tin foil by two giant hands. Ice and snow comprised one hand; fire and sand, the other. Both had seven fingers, each one of them ringed with a rainbow's color. Robert's hands mimicked the actions taking place in the sky as he gazed at a speckled golden orb, as large as the moon. It was an undead eye, spying, peering down at him.

The blackness of space surrounding the sky's eye and hands prevented him from seeing any other features of whatever being was out there. His brain, however, was fully exposed to its view. Before he could even consider the broken-eggshell state of his skull, the golden orb shot down a shaft of light, piercing the gray-matter soil of Robert's brain. His eyesight dimmed as he quivered and intuited the species of this extradimensional creature: *World-Ender*.

The whites of his eyes transmuted into gaseous clouds as his pupils dilated, eradicating the irises, leaving an ultrathin corona at the outer edge as they became like frozen stars—black holes. Time stuttered in his mind. Subconscious thoughts moved at light-speed—leaving whistling and glistening detritus in their wake—as he sensed increasing populations within him, followed swiftly by pollution, cellular degeneration, wild changes in body temperature, and competition among internal windy spirits.

He felt himself being torn and rebuilt with amoral materials; no God or Satan was involved here. The visible and invisible lights of stars and his soul intertwined. He prayed for the peace of death—but his re-creators were probably as deaf as he.

Robert heard the repeated chant *"You...see...reality"* coming from deep within himself. The words bubbled up in the blood rushing to his head.

His vision focused—not as his eyes would have, but more like a remote hovering camera: first on him, then widening to reveal the glowing white spiderweb on which his body lay.

He was stuck. He could move his head and eyes to look around, but his body was otherwise numb, stretched in an "X" position. He couldn't even flinch when he saw the giant orange-and-black metallic spider off to the side, watching him intently. It also didn't move, but something—some *things*—on its body did.

Hundreds of fingernail-sized creatures crawled off of the spider and onto the web, scuttling toward Robert. The little copper-and-ebony metallic creatures were miniature replicas of the giant spider. He closed his eyes as they swarmed his body, hoping whatever they were doing would be over soon.

He opened his eyes when he felt himself moving. The spiders had sheared Robert's outer skin from him. They were now trans-porting him across the web.

"...What you see is reality..."

Their voices tiny and grating, like metal meeting metal, the dime-sized spiders repeated the mantra in unison as they carried his body to the edge of the web. His old skin's husk remained where it was; the giant spider crawled over to it and waited, as if planning to eat it once the rest of Robert was out of sight.

The tiny spiders carried Robert from the web to the ground, dropped their load, and scattered. Having been dumped flat onto his back, it took a moment for Robert to sit up and realize he was in a garden of giant unrecognizable plants and massive objects he presumed to be some sort of vegetables. *No more secret gardens.* He for some reason recalled Artemisia's odd statement as he got to his feet.

His surroundings were strange, but he was stranger. His new skin was semitransparent; through it, Robert saw a slow-swirling green substance making eerie patterns both familiar and unnamable. The skin felt thin, rubbery, and smooth to the touch. He worried just how thin and fragile it really was. If he tripped and fell on his knee or on a rock...He looked at his legs. No genitalia. Wherever he was, he was anatomically incorrect. At least it would make running easier.

He took his first steps forward, on a red clay-brick road wide enough for three or four people to walk abreast. On either side, gigantic plants blocked his view of anything beyond the garden. Behind him, the large spider's web was now uninhabited but impassible. Ahead, the road continued through the garden but stopped at what appeared to be a black wall in the distance. It may've been a dead end, but it seemed the best option.

The sky above wasn't the high and smooth blue he was used to, more like an immense and dangerously deep swimming pool. The watery sky's surface seemed miles above the ground, but large tree roots emerged, dangling and moving like tentacles. Robert stared at them as he walked, not shifting his gaze until he stumbled on a fist-sized ruby lying in the road. He didn't fall, but the near-accident served as a warning that he'd best mind the path.

He strolled at a cautious pace, wondering at the dark wall ahead that got greener and greener as he approached. The plants on either side of him seemed taller as he progressed, their tops hanging over the road, obscuring his view of the sea-sky except for random patches. The patches revealed the tree roots extending their reach downward the farther he went. He walked up an incline, wondering: *If those things are really the tree roots they look like, then just what do the "trees" on the other side of the sea-sky look like? And what exactly are these roots drawing from the air I'm breathing? Or am I breathing? Am I—?*

He tried not to think the obvious. He *couldn't* be dead. He had no other explanation for what this was, but he'd be damned if he had spent seventeen years on Earth accomplishing nothing. Well, hell, maybe that was it. He'd been damned. He hadn't really been given a chance to live, and here he was. Someone owed him answers.

He emerged at the top of a hill and finally saw the dark green wall for what it was—not actually a wall at all. A large, densely wooded area was at the base of the hill. The greenness continued on to a great height, segueing into stout brown tubes that stretched higher before splintering into a dense mass of roots entangling with those descending from the sea-sky. What had seemed like a dark opaque wall from afar was actually a forest of pine trees, unusually thick, incredibly tall, and upside down.

It was impossible to see any sky over the forest. It seemed to stretch up and on forever, deep into the overhead sea. On either side, the trees yawned on into the horizon. Robert had no choice but to walk on through. The red clay-brick road, after all, led straight into it.

Grotesque and foreboding from the outside, the evergreen forest was even creepier inside. It lacked not only sound but animals and even insects. Robert bristled each time the pine needles brushed against his thin, soft skin, but he had no fear of encountering any lions, tigers, or bears. *Alice and Dorothy had their adventures; I guess this one's mine.*

Hell, if his life had been a joke, why not make a joke of his afterlife? But even as he laughed at the idea of it, he had a second thought. Neither Alice nor Dorothy had died. His story may've been just as simple as theirs: He was jogging, tripped, hit his head, and began dreaming while knocked unconscious in the woods. That made the most sense. The trick now was to navigate his way back to rational consciousness before the elements in the real world or his own actions killed him.

He took three quick turns, then found an opening between two trees just a step away. He thought he saw water. He thought he was entering a clearing. Instead, he stood in the middle of a giant mirror. The moment he saw his reflection, the mirror cracked.

Immersed in glass shards and milky darkness, Robert fell like a bowling ball dropped from a skyscraper. He fell for what could've been a minute or an hour, then abruptly stopped, suspended in a spread-eagle position for several moments. Then he fell again, much slower than before. He figured he'd entered a time-trapped slice of space. He again thought of Alice—in Wonderland *and* through the Looking-Glass—before he landed face down on something cushiony.

He turned himself over and sat up. He'd landed on a small mound covered with unusually soft grass. Amazingly, his skin seemed to be unbroken. Around him, he saw giant, prickly flower bushes and, in the distance, something large, long, and tubular weaving between them, getting closer. He froze when he realized what it was. When it was close enough, the monster also stopped.

The creature's head lay on the ground at the foot of the mound. Robert figured it was twice the size of his Mustang as he gazed at its pink eyes, the pits in the nose, and the forked tongue flickering from its mouth. Brown fur covered every area of its body, except the albino head.

The snakelike creature locked on his gaze, flicking its tongue, while Robert considered his escape options. Was this thing his version of Wonderland's rabbit? He couldn't remember how Alice had dealt with that creature, but he had to try something. Anything.

He was on the verge of speaking to the creature when, in a whirlwind of movements, it coiled around the mound and hung its head over him. Robert lost his words. The snake monster's nose-pits were in direct line with Robert's eyes. Before he could even debate his next move, the creature snatched him with its forked tongue and swallowed him whole.

Not only was he unharmed, but Robert didn't even seem to be inside a living creature. Incredibly, he stood on an emerald step of a room he recognized from so many art books, one from M.C. Escher's *Relativity.*

"Welcome to XynKroma. Welcome to the Ground of *Being.*"

The raspy voice came from the center of the emerald room, where wisps of yellow and blue smoke striped the air, enshrouding only parts of the hovering giant. It was as big as the snake's head that had swallowed Robert, but this was only a head. Not that of a bald albino snake, but that of a lynx with green and brown fur. This creature didn't look hungry; it had a more unsettling look in its eyes.

Robert wasn't sure where to start. *XynKroma?* Was that the equivalent of Wonderland, the world behind the Looking Glass, or Purgatory? An insuppressible anxiety pushed him to the easiest question first. "Did you bring me here?"

"I did not bring you to this realm," the lynx said. "You came because you are still looking for yourself. But once you landed, I did guide you *here.* I have been waiting for some time."

Robert took in the entire scope of the emerald room and then the giant head again. "Oz, right?"

"You are no Dorothy," the lynx replied. "More like Job."

Memories flooded Robert's mind, almost too much to handle: his long-ago reading of the Book of Job, Rev. Richardson's more recent sermon and interpretation, and his encounter with

Artemisia. His life lately had certainly been like Job's. Was that it? Was he the subject of a wager between God and Satan?

"Yes," the lynx replied, "and no." One could never tell with a cat's face, even a giant one, but Robert swore the thing was grinning at him. "You see, the story of Job is just that. A story. One of a countless number of stories. Each living being has its own narrative."

It seemed the creature could read his mind, but Robert preferred to speak aloud when asking, "And what's this?" He gestured at his surroundings. "The book cover for my story?"

"This is Ultimate Reality," the lynx said. "XynKroma. The Ground of Being. This dimension is where the Creator's thoughts are most pure before they waft out into your realm, the surface of Reality, which is as far from Reality as one can get."

Robert reassessed his surroundings, giving special attention to the arched portals—up, down, across, and slantwise—all leading outside. He couldn't see any details beyond them, just a golden glow. The portals may've been escapes, or they may've been routes to something worse than the impossible structure where he was. He saw etchings on the walls, like Egyptian hieroglyphs. But the marks weren't drawings of people, eyes, and birds; they were numbers, symbols, and equations.

"Am I dead?"

It came out as a question, but Robert didn't mean it as one. It was more like the whistle blowing in a wrestling match between two sides of his brain. Either he was dead, or this was some grand delusion. Either the time he'd spent in his bedroom was actually him on his deathbed, or—

"Songs, stories, bodily decomposition," the lynx said. "This is what it sounds like when God goes crazy. But you are not dead, yet."

Robert gave the creature his renewed attention.

"Artemisia," he said. "She said something about God going insane."

"Yes, your relative," the lynx said. "She had much to say, some of it true."

"Only some?" Robert was hoping for "None."

"She is correct that your mind and hers share a special connection," the lynx said, "but her mind is twisted; her soul, corrupt. She went through the same Job-like trials and tribulations as you. She was a recipient of the ultimate revelation, the painful one that instructs the chosen of the necessity of leaving friends, family, and even their own bodies behind in order to enter the realm of God. But she did not completely understand what she experienced. She survived afterward, but in order to help her make sense of her world seen with new eyes and a partially enlightened mind, she drafted a narrative about the way things are, basing it off the story she knew best."

"Genesis," Robert said. "Adam and Eve, and Eden."

"The essence of what she told you is true," the lynx said. "What is important—the biggest truth she told you—is that myths, stories, narratives constructed in your realm all have greater weight than you imagine. After all, those creative stories your people tell, and the way they tell them, have to originate from somewhere, right?"

"The realm of the Creator..." Robert considered the Bible and how some took it to be the unblemished word of God. He thought about how the gospels in the New Testament contradicted one another in certain details. And he now remembered an old sermon in which Rev. Richardson explained that there were two contradictory Creation stories in the first couple of chapters of Genesis, one in which man and woman were created together, another where Eve was created after Adam. The stories had been crammed together to make one, and Rev. Richardson had gone into the details of what this meant for Believers, historically and psychologically. That sermon was from so long ago. Robert had been seven years old when he heard it. And, not really caring at the time, he hadn't given it a second thought. Why was he remembering it all now, crystal clear?

"The land of God is the land of memory, among other things," the lynx said. "The Creator's mind is wired to every sentient being. Sentient beings, for lack of a better word, *feed* the Creator with their own narratives, not with prayers. Sentient beings are creative, to put it simply, because of the Creator. As a result, all sentient beings are *touched* in the head, to a greater or lesser extent, because of the Creator."

Robert wondered, between him and Artemisia, who was touched to a greater extent.

"You damaged her badly," the lynx said. "You hit her where it hurts—psychologically. Artemisia is now wandering your realm in a daze. She has temporarily forgotten about you and her own story, but she will remember. She will come back for you."

"Why?"

"Artemisia knows the world will end," the lynx said. "She was correct that Reality is at a tipping point. God will either go completely crazy, or get better. Chaos or a universal Paradise will be the result. And which way the scales tip will depend on a new narrative, one of the strongest stories ever told."

"Didn't happen with Jesus, huh?" Robert knew it was blasphemy to say, but he could hardly help himself. He felt a warm sensation. The green substance within him swirled at a faster rate. Without having moved a step since entering the room, something was tipping his balance.

"The new narrative will be told," the lynx said, "by the child of your mother."

Robert sat down. He'd a feeling all of this was leading to some "chosen one" announcement. Artemisia had started it; this was continuing it. He was too off-balance to receive the news as he felt he should, on his feet with chest out and fists clenched. He could only lean forward, elbows on his knees, and mutter, "Me, huh?"

"No," the lynx said. "The other one."

Robert tightened his fingers into fists as he straightened. "There is no other one." The green substance churned faster, separating into shades of yellow and blue. "You're a damned liar."

"The human mind is a wonderful thing," the lynx said. "It can take you backward and forward in time with memories and hope. It can take you to different realms of Reality. You have had much confusion in your lifetime about your own identity. Being overly judgmental of others has been the result. You have been repressing quite a bit...One memory you have done well in repressing is the fact that your mother was pregnant when she was slain."

Robert released the tension in his hands, but the substance within him didn't slow. It churned and sloshed like water in a washing machine as the blue and yellow became many distinct hues, ranging from sky blue to navy blue, from pale lemon to old gold.

"As she stalked you," the lynx said, "Artemisia kept asking you to *remember*. Did you not wonder why?"

He didn't. He thought she was just being loathsome and creepy. But, now: "Are you saying *she* killed—?"

"She had nothing to do with your mother's demise. But she was after the soul of your mother's child. Her urging you to *remember* was intended to use your mind to turn a combination, one that would open a safe."

"Making me unsafe," Robert mumbled.

"Not only your body and mind," the lynx said, "but your very soul would have been vulnerable. With your psychic connection to her, the right combination would have brought the two of you here, to XynKroma. She would have discovered the truth about your sibling, realized *that* was what she was after, then ripped your soul apart before she fled off to retrieve it."

Robert's world was now being ripped apart. Fitting, he supposed, after what he'd gone through back in his own world. But here close to God, in this new body...his soul. He noticed the substance within it fading to shades of orange and indigo that refused to blend even as they churned faster and he felt warmer. His soul was basically naked in this land of the Creator. The land of hope...and memory.

Robert may have been out of his element, but he could still think. He could still add and subtract. And—Artemisia had been right—he *was* good at abstract thinking. Yes, his mother had been pregnant when she was killed; a cop had told him more than he wanted to hear on that day. And based on what he was hearing now, the baby's soul hadn't gone to Heaven or Hell, nor had it evaporated. It had survived in another realm. *XynKroma.*

He remembered what Artemisia had said about souls dividing, pieces of Eve being buried in another dimension, and Adam.

Artemisia had gotten rid of her other victims by urging them to remember, forcing them to think hard about where they might have seen her before. And while they were looking intently at her, thinking hard, she looked back—straight into their eyes—and thought harder, sending both their souls to XynKroma where she proceeded to wrestle them and, undoubtedly being stronger, ripped their souls apart. If she'd brought Robert here, she would've torn apart both his and his sibling's soul.

His mother had called him a mistake. Essentially, a *bad seed.* But what had she hoped for his sibling? Robert realized his whole life was a narrative, just like every other human being's life was a good story. And *all* of the stories were part of God's ultimate narrative about the war between Paradise and Chaos, the battle for Creation...the battle for God's sanity. But maybe Robert's personal narrative was deeper, more important than others' stories. And maybe that was the root cause of all he'd recently suffered. *Bad seed.* He remembered his vision in the church parking lot.

So, what about his sibling's story? This creature wanted to know it. That's why Robert was here. The realm of *memory* and hope. The lynx was reading Robert, plumbing his soul, unlocking the puzzles of his mind in the hope of finding just *where* in XynKroma his sibling soul might be. The creature was doing the same thing as Artemisia—and a much better job of it.

The substance within Robert shifted its shades to red and violet. The colors battled like the winds and waters of a hurricane. The lynx knew it had been discovered. Each portal in the room sealed itself with stained glass. There was no longer any clear escape route. And the creature seemed to have no more words. It simply gazed at Robert as it shuddered, the head shrinking and floating closer as legs grew out of its throat. *No*— not legs. Tentacles. Ten of them.

Robert knew a threat when he saw one. And at this point, he was as a hot as he could stand. *Don't quit, damn it.*

He gave over to his survival instinct, his dream instinct, and his Warrior wrestler's instinct—a new personal trinity—as his body grew in size, matching the menacing lynx. Robert leapt at it and grabbed two tentacles. The lynx wrapped two others around his torso.

"You cannot win." Two tentacles grabbed Robert's ankles while two others grabbed his wrists.

"Maybe I couldn't win the state of Virginia," Robert said, "but I'll damn sure win the state of my soul."

Sticky filaments—pliable as thread, sharp as needles— undergird each of the tentacles. Robert didn't relinquish the two tentacles he held in his hands, not even when the filaments jabbed and stabbed him, penetrating his thin soul-skin.

He struggled to gain control of something that had no wrists, no ankles, no waist, and no neck, losing hope as his extremities bled red and violet. Each arm fighting him was a taunt. The millions of sharp, sticky threads like every threat and insult he'd ever heard, every injury he'd ever experienced. The lynx was every enemy, human and otherwise, rolled into one.

The fantastic structure around Robert and the lynx trembled as they tussled in the air. The stained windows cracked, but didn't shatter. The staircases shifted their positions, appearing even more impossible by the laws of physics Robert knew. It was like being inside a Rubik's Cube as it solved itself, shrinking itself. The room was folding in.

Robert was at his most vulnerable, but his instincts took notice of his altering surroundings and altered him in turn. His soul shifted its center of gravity and reshaped itself, sprouting more and more limbs that reached and stretched, grappling with the tentacles and wrapping around the lynx's ferocious head. Robert's soul didn't stop at ten; it produced ten times ten—a hundred limbs, many of which wrestled with and whipped against his opponent while the others searched the enfolding structure, tracing the mathematical equations on the folding walls.

The lynx trembled more than the structure surrounding them. It was now struggling. It was now afraid. It had apparently reached the limits of its creativity as it did not or could not reshape itself to meet the threat of Robert's soul, which now looked like nothing less than a spaghetti monster. The lynx fell back to words.

"You are in error," it shouted with a quivering voice. "I am your redeemer. You have to leave your body, friends, and family behind...That is the cost of Paradise. You—"

Robert didn't care for its gibberish. He tuned it out as he garnered new ideas from the mathematical equations he read like braille. While the room folded down to the size of a classroom, Robert reached and whipped his limbs in one beautiful combination—grabbing the creature in ninety-nine different spots, penetrating, retracting—*ripping* the creature into a million pieces with one swift movement.

Robert watched the torn pieces fall like snow, fading from luminous green to indigo to violet to nothing. For at least another moment, his soul was safe, if not redeemed. The room's collapse could mean death for him, with no afterlife.

He thought of his mom…his beautiful mother. Maybe all these years he'd been subconsciously blaming her in the same way so many had been blaming Eve. He still had a lot of work to do. If he survived, he'd investigate the fate of his sibling's soul on his own terms, in his own time, in one realm or another, but *alone*. That's how he would find his redemption. That's how he would find the ending to his story. That's how he might contribute, in the most positive way, to the Creator's great narrative.

For now all he had was an epiphany: the diving into oneself brought more horrors than any monster, creature, or alien from without could ever deliver, but such an internal journey is necessary for discovering the fundamental truth of one's humanity.

As the room crumpled in on itself and the stained glass burst in flashes of innumerable colors, Robert was overcome by a cacophony of noises and voices—bizarre, brilliant, and beautiful. *Time, untie me.* He hoped to live beyond the implosion and have the strength to go further.

His body lay on its side, on a small patch of damp grass in a clearing encircled by trees. With both hands on his ears and knees touching his chest, he resembled a human question mark, failing in its attempt to become a zero.

The noontime sun shined overhead, warming the area, melting the lingering ice and snow. One open eye gazed upward. The other wasn't open but, like a well-positioned movie camera, it saw him. It saw his immediate surroundings. And, before fading to black, it saw three men and one woman approaching.

Robert was alive. He was in his own realm. And he was still plagued.

His open eye continued to gaze toward the sun, until another bright circle entered his range of vision. A bronze badge, attached on the heart side of a man's black jacket. The letters H.S.A. were at its center.

Robert deduced his next destination as his eye closed. Mathematical equations painted themselves in gold on the black canvas of his consciousness.

Read on for an excerpt from the first book
in the *Eve of Light* series:

Broken Angels

BROKEN ANGELS

CHAPTER ONE

Robert Goldner bent the light around his body, making himself invisible.

No alarms went up. Better, no gang signals. The kids stayed put. They appeared to be minding nobody's business, just waiting for the day of reckoning. Eight years after the emergence of the White Fire Virus, though, Robert damn well knew the younger the potential threat, the greater the potential danger.

It was a Friday afternoon in September, and none of the kids seemed to have anything better to do. The nine boys and two girls probably should've been in...junior high school, from the looks of it. But they were hanging out in front of a pizza place and a check-cashing shop. Smoking, joking around, dressed like thugs-in-training. Robert wondered if they were just truants or if they were staking out territory early, waiting for the needy folks who were done with their workweek to come by and cash their paychecks. Big kids, or little criminals?

Hard to tell what anyone was really up to these days. Easier not to trust anyone.

Six, seven, maybe even eight years their senior, Robert could probably take them. But he didn't like fighting kids, even if they thought they were adults, even if such confrontations came with the territory of being a Watcher. Anyway, he needed to conserve his strength for the hunt.

He maneuvered through the cluster, none of the kids suspecting a thing. The parasites inside Robert may've been slowly killing him, but thank fortune they didn't leave him defenseless. He stayed invisible as he ran on toward the target house, five blocks away.

Generations have trod, have trod, have trod...

Funny—lines from Hopkins's poem about the grandeur of God often shot through his thoughts during this part of the hunt. The poet had surely seen his share of wretched scenes from the big picture of a downtrodden human family and its ravished home. Hopkins may not have witnessed as many underpass-and bus-stop-dwelling Jellyheads, the shit-and-piss-stenched fiends of no permanent residence strung out on Jelly Raptures, sprawled out amid the irrepressible scatterings of condom wrappers, broken beer bottles, 7-Eleven chili dog boxes, and all the rest of it, but life wasn't all that wonderful one hundred and fifty years ago either. Still, Robert couldn't bring himself to share the poet's optimism that "nature is never spent."

Oh, well—"Don't Worry, Be Happy."

Funny how he often recalled the lines of that dumb rhyme during these hunts as well.

What was the worry anyway? The odds were against his surviving to witness humankind's last day. He could die within the next few seconds, stopped cold on the way to potentially winning this week's mystery prize. He might even be successful and come out a hero, only to have the billions of parasitic microbes living in his skin and blood cells kill him shortly afterward. *Generations have trod, have trod, have trod...*

This one was a long shot, he'd been told. Probably a Friday afternoon wild goose chase. But he was never one to waste time. On the sidewalk and across lawns, he moved as fast as he could in jeans and a windbreaker. If he'd been wearing less, he could've moved even faster, gliding over the ground, skating on thin air. But, invisible or not, he wasn't about to strip down to his drawers.

It had nothing to do with shyness. He'd never been accused of being infected with modesty. It was his actual infection that was the problem. Baring too much skin to light was equivalent to inviting the parasites within to feast—get drunk then unruly. Hopefully, though, never to the extent of what he saw when he rounded the corner.

Robert had actually heard the sound of it first, the labored breathing like the sound of a large sack of junk being dragged slowly over a gravel road. Even in silence, he would not have missed seeing the man, naked except for his underwear, socks, and one shoe, propped up against the blue postal box in front of a seemingly deserted apartment complex.

The man didn't have much further to go. Even from forty feet away, Robert could see the patches of skin that had fallen off, patches matching the thinness, brittleness, and colors—if not exactly the size—of maple leaves in autumn. It was a clear day, and the sun shined freely. The parasites had overdosed, and the man was being eaten away, rapidly, by the frantic microbes inside him. The Virus was claiming him, overtaking him, exposing more and more of his insides to the outside world, the world empty of anyone who'd see—except invisible Robert.

The man was beyond blind at this point. But Robert remained unseen as he studied him, approaching ever more cautiously lest the leaking radiation resulting from the man's death throes envelope him, causing the parasites within Robert's body to go ballistic.

No more than a dozen skin patches had fallen from the dying man, and what was still hanging on was turning the hue of rice paper, or the color and texture of tree bark, dotted all over with dark silver glitter that sparkled from black to red to orange to yellow to green to blue to indigo to violet and then briefly to silver before going back to black, each piece of glitter sparking through the color-cycle at its own unique pace.

Robert had seen it all before. It wasn't all that shocking. He did briefly wonder what Hopkins might think of this Pied Ugly; certainly not "Glory be to God for dappled things—" But Robert's brief imagining turned back to stark reality as he stepped nearer, looked closer, and saw something unusual.

The man still had skin covering most of his abdominal area. Robert concentrated and pushed his vision down the spectrum into the range of x-rays, trying to figure why the wheezing man's stomach appeared be getting redder than a cranberry as it swelled more and more with each breath.

Robert saw through the layers of skin and muscle. He saw the man's intestines breaking all of their bodily connections to form one long worm.

Part of him wanted to wretch, but Robert couldn't take his eye away.

A chunky vomit, looking like milk four weeks past its expiration date, oozed out of the left side of the man's mouth as the intestine-worm thrashed violently in the limited space provided to it inside the self-destructing body. It didn't take long for the thing to find pathways around rotten, mushy organs and bones that were more flexible than pipe cleaners, the head and tail of it writhing and wriggling in opposite directions as it searched for freedom.

In his time, Robert had seen a lot that was fantastic and horrific, but when one end of the intestine-worm wriggled out of man's anus as the other end simultaneously wriggled out of his mouth, he almost lost it—his consciousness, if not his sanity.

Robert backpedaled and turned, almost tripping over his own feet, then trotted a few steps more to regain his balance. Covering his mouth and nose with the inside of his right elbow, he put three fingers on the face of his right-wristwatch. The man was dead, but it would be nice to have the authorities swing by and pick up the body before some roving hooligans found it and did who knows what with it.

After transmitting the message to his superior, Robert glanced back once more at the corpse. There but for the grace of medication goes he.

Robert shook his head to stop his full-body shudder then continued on his way.

He ran just under a sprint until he came to the quiet, middle-class neighborhood. He slowed, paying extra-special attention to his surroundings as he jogged toward the target house. It had a manicured lawn, an empty driveway, a wreathed front door, and plenty of windows—with closed blinds. Blinds Robert couldn't see through, with or without his x-raying vision. This wasn't another Friday-afternoon wild goose chase.

He used his right-wristwatch to contact his superior again. Robert had a hunch, a good one, and he needed backup—a few cops, some FBI agents, or something even better. The superior's response: all official authorities were occupied elsewhere. Something about gunfire and explosions in the area of Pentagon City. Robert and his partner would have to handle this hunt, together and alone.

Sure. His partner. The partner who should've been by his side since daybreak. The partner Robert hadn't seen since the day before. Just a little more than a year older than Robert, he wasn't acting much better than the truants on the street corner, minding nobody's business.

Robert used his left-wristwatch to send his partner a message he knew would go unanswered. He then continued his reconnaissance.

As the minutes passed, his sense of dread increased. Whatever story was hidden inside that house, it was one full of terror, and one eager to be told. Robert would have to make a decision, soon, about whether he was willing to hear it alone.

ABOUT THE SERIES

Eve of Light is a Dark Metaphysical Fantasy series chronicling the surreal events leading up to the Apocalypse—the Death of God. The setting is a contemporary, alternate Earth on the verge of a cataclysm that will warp space, time, and minds. The main narrative of those plotting and battling to save humanity is told in the *Eve of Light* series of novels. The short stories and novellas are simply flashes on the fringe—episodes told from the perspective of everyday men and women living in a world turned weird.

The Core Novels
> BloodLight: The Apocalypse of Robert Goldner
> Broken Angels *(Eve of Light * Book I)*
> Divinities, Entangled *(Eve of Light * Book II)*

Stories on the Fringe
> FoolKillers
> The Lark
> Heaven's Gun
> Knotty & Ice
> Rogue Beauty
> Deviant-Hunter's Sabbath

ABOUT THE AUTHOR

Harambee K. Grey-Sun writes under the broad umbrella of speculative fiction. He integrates elements of fantasy, horror, noir, black humor, and science fiction into his work and spins dark, surreal, mysterious, grotesque, at times challenging, and often blasphemous tales. Many of his stories can be categorized into one or more of the following subgenres: speculative thriller, urban fantasy, metaphysical fantasy, superhero, occult/supernatural, slipstream, and–*of course*–weird fiction. His Dark Metaphysical Fantasy series *Eve of Light* examines the dark nature of God and what it really means to be human.

For more information:

Click Here for Author's Website
www.harambeegreysun.com